FROM THE
NANCY DREW FILES

THE CASE: Nancy sets out to clear the air at a ski resort—and clear the name of a girl accused of embezzlement.

CONTACT: George's friend Rebecca Montgomery is fired by Tall Pines when the owner finds some of the stolen money in her purse.

SUSPECTS: Karl Reismueller—the owner of Tall Pines says Rebecca stole his money, but he refuses to bring the police in to investigate.

Jody Ashton—one day the manager of the ski shop is complaining about her pay, the next day she's driving to work in a new sports car.

Ben Wrobley—the ski instructor resents that he wasn't chosen to run the ski school, and he's determined to make Tall Pines pay.

COMPLICATIONS: George has fallen for one of the suspects, Ben Wrobley, and she may have revealed Nancy's true identity—putting them both in danger.

Books in The Nancy Drew Files® Series

Available from ARCHWAY Paperbacks

THE
NANCY DREW
FILES™

Case 64

THE WRONG TRACK

CAROLYN KEENE

AN ARCHWAY PAPERBACK
Published by POCKET BOOKS
New York   London   Toronto   Sydney   Tokyo   Singapore

This book is a work of fiction. Names, characters, places and incidents are either the product of the author's imagination or are used fictitiously. Any resemblance to actual events or locales or persons, living or dead, is entirely coincidental.

AN ARCHWAY PAPERBACK *Original*

An Archway Paperback published by
POCKET BOOKS, a division of Simon & Schuster Inc.
1230 Avenue of the Americas, New York, NY 10020

Copyright © 1991 by Simon & Schuster Inc.
Produced by Mega-Books of New York, Inc.

ISBN: 0-671-73068-1

First Archway Paperback printing October 1991

10 9 8 7 6 5 4 3 2

NANCY DREW, AN ARCHWAY PAPERBACK and colophon are registered trademarks of Simon & Schuster Inc.

THE NANCY DREW FILES is a trademark of Simon & Schuster Inc.

Cover art by Tom Galasinski

Printed in the U.S.A.

IL 6+

THE WRONG TRACK

Chapter

One

"Wow!" Nancy Drew exclaimed, peering out the window at the snow swirling in wintry gusts. "It's really coming down!"

"That's terrific," her friend George Fayne said from where she lay sprawled on her living room floor, a bowl of popcorn at her elbow. "The trails at Tall Pines could use it," she said.

Nancy brushed her silky reddish blond hair behind her ears and pulled her royal blue sweater tight around her. "You've got skiing on the brain," Nancy joked, turning to face her friend.

"She sure does," Bess Marvin, George's cousin, agreed from the sofa. "Pass the popcorn, George."

"What about your diet?" George grinned.

Bess tossed back her long blond hair and snatched at the bowl. "It's low-cal," she insisted, popping a handful into her mouth. "No butter."

1

Nancy smiled at Bess and George. For cousins, they couldn't be less alike. Dark-haired George was tall with an athlete's slim build. She was into bicycling and skiing. Bess was short and blond, and the sports she was most into were shopping and trying to stick to the latest fad diet.

"Are you guys ready to watch this?" George asked, holding up a videocassette. She read out loud from the back of the box. " 'Tall Pines—the Midwest's newest, biggest, most luxurious cross-country ski resort. State-of-the-art trails. Fully loaded exercise rooms. Spa. Sauna. Three-star restaurant and lodge—' "

"Now those last two I could go for," Bess said, reaching for the video.

George held it away from her. " 'Private banquet rooms for conventions. Heated indoor pool.' "

"This place sounds like too much," Nancy said. She plopped down on the floor next to George to study the picture on the cassette box. Nestled in a deep valley of thick green pines, Tall Pines lived up to its name. The complex—which consisted mainly of cedar and glass buildings—was beautiful. "I can see why you want to work there," Nancy said to George.

George popped the cassette into the VCR and pressed Play. "I know I can teach skiing, and as soon as I memorize this video, there's no way they won't hire me!"

"What ever happened to Rob Watson's place?" Bess asked, stifling a yawn.

Bess was referring to a resort north of River

Heights where George had always gone cross-country skiing before.

"What about Watson's trails?" Nancy asked George. "Aren't they as good?"

George shrugged, her eyes glued to the TV screen as the video came on. "Sure. I guess the trails are as good, but Rob hasn't got all the extra stuff Tall Pines has."

As Nancy watched the video, she saw that George was right. She'd been to Rob's a few times, and it couldn't begin to compare to the luxury Tall Pines had to offer. Rob's was basically just a few trails and a snack bar. Nancy wondered if he was losing business to the new resort already.

She was about to ask George when the doorbell rang. George stopped the video and got up to answer the front door.

Nancy could spy a tall, brown-haired girl talking to George in the hallway. The girl seemed upset, and George was trying to calm her down. Finally she put an arm around the girl and led her into the living room.

"Nancy, Bess," George said, "this is Rebecca Montgomery. Rebecca, this is my friend Nancy Drew and my cousin Bess Marvin."

"Nice to meet you," Rebecca said, her voice unsteady. She was very pretty, with intense brown eyes and a cascade of soft brown hair. Dropping her purse from her shoulder to her hand, Rebecca perched on a nearby rocking chair.

George sat down next to Bess on the sofa.

"Rebecca hooked me up with the guy who's interviewing at Tall Pines."

Rebecca smiled a little, but Nancy was watching her hands as they twisted nervously in her lap. The girl was obviously upset.

"Rebecca's in trouble," George said softly, confirming Nancy's suspicions. "I told her you might be able to help."

"What kind of trouble?" Nancy asked.

"Should I tell them, or do you want to?" George asked Rebecca.

The girl swallowed a few times. "You go ahead," she said, unzipping her black and white parka. Shivering slightly, she held her hands out toward the warm blaze in the fireplace.

"Tell us what?" Bess asked, her blue eyes round with curiosity.

"Rebecca works in the office at Tall Pines." George ran her hands through her short, curly brown hair. "Or used to work there. She got fired."

Nancy saw Rebecca flinch at the word *fired*. "What happened?" Nancy asked.

"Someone stole fifty thousand dollars from the resort's safe," Rebecca moaned, "and left two thousand of it in my purse!"

"Oh, no!" Bess exclaimed softly.

"I didn't do it," Rebecca said to Nancy. "I didn't steal that money."

"Of course you didn't," George put in. She rested her elbows on her knees and squinted, deep in thought. "But somebody sure wants to make it look like you're a thief."

4

Nancy hopped up and began to pace the room, her arms crossed in front of her. Her detective instincts were on red alert, and her mind raced with questions.

"What happened, exactly?" Nancy asked politely.

Rebecca took a deep breath and plunged in. "I'm the bookkeeper at Tall Pines. It's my first job out of school. I'm lucky to have it"— Rebecca paused—"or at least I *was* lucky." Her eyes dropped to her lap. "Oh, what am I going to do?" she said suddenly, tears filling her eyes.

"Nancy'll help," Bess assured her. "She's a crack detective and will find out what happened."

Bess beamed at Nancy, and Nancy wished her friend hadn't said she'd take the case. That should be her decision to make. "Thanks for the vote of confidence," she said graciously to Bess anyway. She turned to Rebecca. "Tell us about it. Take your time."

Rebecca nodded, wiped the tears from her eyes, and went on. "The computerized payroll system wasn't working, so we had a lot of cash in the safe in Dave's office to pay the employees. Fifty thousand dollars, to be exact. The same afternoon that the money disappeared, three weeks ago, two thousand dollars of it turned up in my purse. I was so shocked when I found it, I didn't know what to do. I did report it, though—" Rebecca broke down again.

"And they accused you?" Nancy guessed.

Rebecca nodded her head slightly. "Not right

away, but Karl Reismueller—he's the owner of Tall Pines—told me this morning that the police and the insurance investigators both decided that there's enough evidence to indicate I could be involved. The serial numbers on the money I found in my purse matched the numbers on the money missing from the safe. And none of the other money has turned up!

"Reismueller said he wouldn't press charges against me," Rebecca continued, the words spilling from her now. "He doesn't want the publicity. He did say he had to fire me, and he wouldn't give me a reference, either."

"That's terrible," Bess said, biting on a fingernail. "You'll have a really hard time getting another job without a reference."

Rebecca swallowed several times. "Don't I know it," she said. "You've got to help me. If I don't work, I can't pay back my student loans."

George got up and went over to Rebecca. "Don't worry." She put a hand on the girl's shoulder. "Nancy will help, won't you, Nan?"

"You bet I will," she said, happy with her decision now. "You've got to start at the beginning and tell me everything. And I mean everything."

Late the next morning Nancy was ready to pull her blue Mustang out of her driveway with George, Bess, and Rebecca there to see her off.

"See you later!" George said with a wave. "And I've decided not to try for a job while we're there. I'll just be a guest."

Bess grinned and pulled her bright red beret down over her blond hair. "Don't forget—we've never seen you before in our lives!"

Nancy laughed and shifted the car into reverse. "Don't worry, Rebecca," she called out the window. "We'll find the real thief, and you'll have your job back in no time."

Rebecca smiled wanly. "Good luck," she called back.

Before heading off Nancy took one last look at her friends. They'd be seeing one another later, but she'd be undercover and have to pretend not to know them. Instead of Nancy Drew, teen detective, she was going to the resort as Nancy Drew, teen reporter for *Tracks,* a cross-country skiing magazine.

After hearing Rebecca's story the previous day Nancy had realized that she wouldn't get anywhere investigating without a cover. Apparently Karl Reismueller had decided Rebecca was the thief, and that was that. The police had closed their investigation, since Reismueller wasn't going to press charges.

When Nancy decided to go undercover, her father, Carson Drew, arranged a cover story with an editor of *Tracks.* Tall Pines was expecting her and would have all kinds of tours and lessons planned for her week's stay. The publicity in *Tracks* would be good for the new resort.

Bess and George were coming up later in the day, and they were going to stay at Tall Pines, too. But Nancy would have to pretend she didn't know them.

As she pulled her Mustang onto the highway that led north to Tall Pines Nancy smiled to herself. It was a great day for a drive. The roads had been plowed, and the two hours it would take to get to Tall Pines should be time enough to plan her strategy. After Rebecca's explanation the day before, Nancy was more sure than ever that the girl hadn't stolen the money. Anyone with forty-eight thousand dollars wouldn't be so worried about how to pay off student loans. But then who had taken the cash?

Nancy mentally went over the short list of names Rebecca had given her: Dave Kendall, Rebecca's boss and the manager of Tall Pines; Karl Reismueller, the owner; Ben Wrobley, a ski instructor; and Jody Ashton, a friend of Rebecca's who ran the ski shop.

According to Rebecca, Ben and Jody had been in her office the morning of the theft. They had come by to see if their pay envelopes were ready. Dave and Karl both had offices next to Rebecca's, and supposedly they were the only ones who knew the combination to the safe where the money was kept.

Still, any one of them could have taken the fifty thousand dollars and stashed two thousand dollars of it in Rebecca Montgomery's purse, especially since Rebecca had left the office at least twice that day. One time she had had to drop off a computer printout at the front desk, and the second time Dave had asked her to take an envelope over to Karl Reismueller's condo.

Nancy stopped thinking about the money and

turned on the radio. It felt great to be back on a case, even if she had to work alone. What she wouldn't give to have Ned with her, though. Ned Nickerson, her longtime boyfriend, was away at college, and she saw too little of him during the school year.

A full-blown image of Ned popped into her mind just then. She could almost feel his strong arms around her, his breath on her face, his lips . . .

The sound of a horn blaring sent Nancy's foot to the brake. She had drifted over into the far lane. Better be more careful, Nancy told herself as she steered the Mustang back. Save thinking about Ned until after you've solved the mystery.

A couple of hours later Nancy turned onto a narrow, winding country road that was far more picturesque than the highway. After less than half an hour Nancy was turning into the entrance of the resort. The private drive curved gently away from the road and was lined with tall pines, their shapes softened into white triangles by the fresh snow.

Nancy drove past the parking lot to the main lodge. "Wow!" she said to herself softly.

The resort was even more breathtaking in real life than on the video. All of the buildings were made of cedar and glass, and no two were identical. A two-story lodge dominated the complex. Nancy pulled to a stop in front of the lodge, slipped on her green parka, and slid her hands into mittens that matched the purple stripe on her green ski pants.

Her car was driven to the visitor parking lot by an employee as she made her way inside. "Wow again," she whispered, taking in the wide expanses of glass that flooded the area with light and gave awesome views of the surrounding pines. At the back of the room a dozen guests were sitting in twos and threes at tables around a roaring fireplace. To her left the registration desk bustled with activity. Along the same wall as the fireplace Nancy noticed a large display window filled with colorful ski clothing. A hand-lettered sign told her it was part of the Tall Pines Gift Shop.

Within a few minutes Nancy had checked in, leaving her luggage with a bellhop. The clerk at the registration desk directed her to the Tall Pines offices and said Dave Kendall was waiting for her there.

"If you go out the front, the administration building is directly across from us," the clerk explained. "You can't miss it."

Nancy thanked him. She had no trouble finding the small A-frame building across from the main lodge. She closed the door behind her and looked around. After the bustle and noise of the crowded main lodge, the offices were eerily silent. She was in the reception area, and there were two doors off a main hallway to her right. One, she knew from Rebecca's description, was Dave's office, where Rebecca had also had her desk. The other was Reismueller's.

Before Nancy could knock on either door, the one on the right flew open.

10

"I know what's going on here," a dark-haired young man with a muscular build shouted as he stormed out of the office. Nancy caught his angry expression and saw that his fists were clenched at his sides.

She heard the deep rumble of a voice responding to the young man but couldn't make out the words.

"If you think I won't tell anyone," the dark-haired young man yelled, shaking his fist, "you're wrong, Dave Kendall. Dead wrong!"

Chapter

Two

THE ANGRY YOUNG MAN strode past Nancy without seeing her. He was about to storm out the front door when an older man with brown hair came running after him.

"Come back here, Ben!" the older man yelled. "You can't go around making accusations like that."

Nancy stood still. Ben? She wondered if the dark-haired young man with the muscular build was Ben Wrobley.

"That's where you're wrong, Kendall!" the young man shouted. Without waiting for an answer he flung open the front door and strode outside, letting the door slam behind him.

For a moment there was silence. Then Nancy cleared her throat. "I'm Nancy Drew," she told the older man. "The desk clerk told me you were expecting me. I can come back later if this is a bad time."

The man smiled and extended his hand to shake Nancy's. "Come right on in, Ms. Drew. I'm Dave Kendall, general manager here at Tall Pines."

So this was Rebecca's former boss, Nancy thought. Taking a closer look, she judged Kendall to be in his midthirties, his brown hair graying at the temples. Though his voice was cordial, she could sense the anger just beneath his perfect smile.

"Let me apologize for what you just overheard," Kendall said, leading the way down the hall to his office. "That young man can get a bit overexcited."

Nancy nodded noncommittally but kept her thoughts to herself as Dave led the way into his office. The room was large and bright, with three skylights cut into the roof. The furniture consisted of two ultramodern desks, several chairs, and a row of matching filing cabinets. On top of the center filing cabinet was a huge vase of orchids. Kendall caught Nancy looking at them.

"My passion," he confessed. "I love fresh flowers." He motioned Nancy to a chair in front of his desk. "We're so glad you're here at Tall Pines. A write-up in *Tracks* is just what a new business needs." Dave leaned back in his chair. Though he appeared relaxed, Nancy felt the tension in him left over from his encounter with Ben. Nancy wondered just what kind of accusation Ben had been making, and if it involved the theft.

"It looks to me as though Tall Pines is doing pretty well," Nancy commented, remembering her cover.

"That's true. We are," Dave admitted, smiling. "But I want to make sure people come back. Resorts depend on repeat customers as well as new ones." The resort manager paused, and his tension seemed to ease as he continued talking. "I'm proud of this resort," he said with conviction. "Tall Pines isn't an average cross-country ski place."

"No, it's not," Nancy agreed. "How many guests can Tall Pines accommodate?" she asked, taking out a notebook and scanning the list of questions she'd prepared.

Kendall's smile was wide and proud. "We're an intimate place. There are one hundred condos, as well as one hundred rooms in the lodge. Skiers who come here know the trails won't be crowded. They appreciate that and pay well for the special treatment we offer. I've put together a packet of brochures for you. They should answer any of your general questions."

Nancy was about to comment when she heard the door to the lobby open and the sound of boots stomping off snow.

Dave stood up and walked to his door. "Good morning, Karl," he called to the newcomer. "Nancy Drew is here."

"Good day," said a deep voice. Nancy turned in her chair and watched a tall man stride into the room. He bowed from the waist in greeting. "I'm Karl Reismueller." As Nancy rose to shake hands with the owner of Tall Pines he took her hand in his and shook it gently.

"Welcome to Tall Pines, Ms. Drew," Karl added in a voice that bore a slight German accent. "I hope you will enjoy your stay here." He ran a hand through his blond hair, which had distinguished wings of silver at the temples.

Nancy smiled. "I'm very glad to be here, Mr. Reismueller," she said honestly.

Karl sat on the edge of the desk and faced Nancy, staring at her intently with his crystal-blue eyes. "Call me Karl, please."

"Karl," Nancy said, blushing. Reismueller really knew how to turn on the charm.

"I would have liked to have given you a tour of Tall Pines myself," Karl went on, "but I have some pressing business matters." He gestured with his right hand. "I've asked an employee, Jody Ashton, to take you around. She manages the gift shop and the ski shop and knows Tall Pines very well."

Jody was Rebecca's friend, Nancy remembered. She'd also been in the office the day of the theft. Nancy smiled to herself that she was able to spend a couple of hours with her.

Nancy thanked Karl. "From what I've seen, Tall Pines is extremely beautiful," she said.

"Once you get out on the trails you'll see the real Tall Pines," Dave told Nancy. "We'll get you fitted with some of our best skis, and you can check out the trails."

"That'll be great," Nancy said.

"Wonderful!" Karl said with a smile, glancing at his watch. "And now I'm afraid I must excuse myself. I'm expecting an important phone call," he explained. He stood up and took Nancy's hand in his once more. "I hope you'll join my wife and me for dinner this evening at the Edelweiss, which is our largest restaurant. Would eight o'clock be convenient?"

Nancy nodded, and Karl left them. Dave studied his own watch. "Let's find Jody," he said, putting on a forest-green down jacket. As he turned to pick up his gloves Nancy saw the Tall Pines logo—two pine trees—emblazoned on the back of the jacket.

Dave led the way back to the main lodge and into the gift shop that Nancy had noticed when she registered. As they entered chimes announced their arrival.

A girl with short, curly auburn hair stepped out from behind the counter. "Hi, Dave," she said, smiling at them. "And you must be Nancy Drew. Karl told me you'd be coming."

"This is Jody Ashton," Dave told Nancy. Jody had a slim, athletic build, the greenest eyes Nancy had seen, long black lashes, and high, aristocratic cheekbones. She was dressed in an oversize wool sweater with the Tall Pines emblem and a pair of matching forest green warm-up pants.

"I'd better get back to the office," Dave said. He gave Nancy a smile that didn't quite reach his eyes. "I'm sure you'll have more questions. When you do, you know where to find me."

Nancy thanked him, and Dave left. She turned to Jody, who appeared to be nervous as she blinked several times.

"I don't know what to say," Jody finally managed to get out, giving Nancy a forced smile. "I've never met a reporter before."

Nancy grinned. "I promise not to write anything incriminating about you," she joked.

Jody seemed afraid for a second and then laughed nervously. "Let me get my jacket, and I'll show you around," she said.

Nancy waited while Jody found her cap and gloves and told the girl she was working with that she'd be leaving for a while.

"This way," Jody said, pointing to a door that opened directly to the outside. She led the way back to the front of the lodge. "That's the Edelweiss," she said, gesturing to a second-story deck that jutted out above the lodge. "If you have a chance to eat there, take it. The food is out of this world."

They walked toward a large building with one solid wall of glass. Inside Nancy could spy an Olympic-size pool. "Wow!" she said.

Pushing open the front door of the building, Jody led the way into the exercise complex. "Neat, huh?" she said. "The pool's still not filled with water," she explained. "It was supposed to be open yesterday, but now they're promising it'll be ready this afternoon."

Nancy followed Jody. From inside the pool room she found herself looking out onto a forest of stately pines that stretched to the sky.

Jody was already walking around the pool to a pair of doors along one side of the wall. "The locker rooms are here," she said, leading the way. "Women's locker room," Jody pointed out, "private showers, fully stocked with all-natural bath and beauty products."

The lavender and forest green locker room, equipped with thick towels and expensive bath products, was much fancier than any locker room Nancy had ever seen. Jody smiled at her. "Our guests want luxury, and they get it. There's also a sauna and an exercise room," Jody told Nancy. "Both coed. Now if you'll follow me, I'll show you one of Tall Pines's most popular attractions."

Outside the girls made their way up a narrow path that had been shoveled in the fresh snow. A short distance from the building Nancy saw steam rising from among a grove of pine trees.

"What's that?" she asked Jody.

"Check it out," Jody said with a raised eyebrow.

Nancy laughed out loud when she discovered the source of the steam. It was an outdoor hot tub with a couple of people in it. "I'm definitely going to make time for this," she declared.

Jody laughed. "I thought you'd like it." She led Nancy down a tree-lined driveway, pointing out a one-story, modern wooden building on their right. "Some of the staff live here," she said. "A lot of employees commute, but some live too far away."

"Do you live here?" Nancy asked.

"No. I live in an apartment in Monroe with my mother. It's a little town about ten minutes away." Jody smiled, showing her pearly, even teeth, and pointed to her left. "That path leads to a frozen pond. It should be great skating, and it will even be lit at night. It's not quite done yet but will be soon."

Nancy followed Jody along a road that curved around the lodge. At the back of the curve Nancy caught sight of a cluster of A-frame buildings in a small clearing. Like the main lodge, each one had a second-story deck and wide expanses of glass.

"Awesome!" Nancy exclaimed. "These must be the condos." Jody nodded. "They're gorgeous. I can see why Mr. Reismueller is so proud of them."

"Then you've met Karl," Jody said, her striking green eyes flashing.

"He was very charming."

"Let me guess." Jody chuckled. "He played his German prince role: the accent, dinner with him and Sheila, the whole bit."

Nancy laughed and took a key from her purse. "You guessed right," she said, checking the number on the key. "I think this one's mine."

They had stopped at the third building. "Karl Reismueller is a walking gold mine," Jody went on. "He has more businesses than I can count, and they're all successful."

As they entered her condo Nancy whistled

softly. "This is fabulous!" The main living area was thickly carpeted and had a huge fireplace that dominated the back wall. A bedroom, kitchenette, and bath completed the first floor, and a sleeping loft filled the second story. There were flowers everywhere, Nancy saw, remembering Dave Kendall's weakness for them.

"No wonder Mr. Reismueller is so successful," Nancy said. "He certainly knows how to treat his guests."

"He could take some lessons on how to treat his employees," Jody said half aloud.

Nancy turned, struck by the bitterness in Jody's voice. "Oh, really?"

Jody's face flushed with embarrassment. "That's off the record," she said.

"No problem," Nancy told her, mentally storing the item away. She glanced at her luggage, which the bellman had brought in, and decided to unpack later. "I'd like to go pick out my skis."

"Sure," Jody said, leading the way back to the rear of the main lodge. "There's the school, and next to it is where we rent equipment," Jody told her. "There's a snack bar, too. The food's good but cheap. Most of the employees eat there."

Nancy took the opportunity to turn the conversation to Rebecca. "I heard you lost an employee recently. Didn't your bookkeeper leave?"

Jody stared at Nancy, her green eyes suddenly angry. "Rebecca didn't leave. She was fired. Personally, I think she probably deserved it."

"What do you mean?" Nancy asked, surprised by Jody's sudden hostility.

Before Jody could answer, a girl ran up to them. "Jody! There you are! I've been looking all over for you." She stopped next to Nancy and Jody. "Michelle's having a problem with the cash register, and she's got customers waiting."

Jody turned to Nancy. "Will you excuse me for a minute? I'll meet you at the ski shop as soon as I'm done."

As Nancy walked slowly toward the shop she tried to make sense of Jody's anger. Why was she so hostile toward Rebecca? Rebecca thought Jody was her friend. If so, Nancy would have expected her to be sympathetic toward Rebecca.

Unless Jody was the person who framed Rebecca, Nancy thought as she stomped the snow off her boots before entering the ski shop and ski school complex. The sign above her head told her that the shop was to the left and the Inge Gustafson Ski School was to the right. Jody seemed friendly enough, but Nancy had learned not to be taken in by charm. And Jody *had* acted nervous when Nancy had jokingly commented about not writing anything incriminating.

Inside, the entrance alcove seemed dark after the dazzling sunshine on the clean snow. Her eyes took a minute to adjust to the darkness.

"I'm sick and tired of this setup!" Nancy heard a masculine voice declare in the ski school to her right.

She stopped. She'd heard that voice before.

"Unless something changes soon," the man went on, "you'd better start looking for another sucker."

Nancy heard what sounded like the thump of a fist on wood. "I'm not going to put up with this much longer." There was no doubt about it. The voice belonged to the same young man who had been shouting at Dave less than an hour before.

"I've got choices," he reminded his listener. "I can always work at Rob Watson's. At least *he's* honest."

Chapter

Three

N**ANCY'S EYES WIDENED.** Twice now she'd heard the dark-haired young man making threats about something that was going on at Tall Pines. She drew in a deep breath and stepped out of the alcove and into the ski school, resolving to find out what he knew.

When she saw that the young man was shouting at Karl Reismueller she was shocked. The two men were standing next to a black potbellied stove. The young man's face was red with anger.

Reismueller spotted Nancy first. "Come in, Nancy," he said, his voice honey smooth and charming. He gestured toward the tall, black-haired young man. "Have you met Ben Wrobley? Ben, this is Nancy Drew, a reporter from *Tracks* magazine," he added importantly. "Ben's one of our best ski instructors."

Ben's shoulders stiffened. He glared at Karl before reaching out to shake hands with Nancy. "Nice to meet you," he said gruffly.

Nancy's investigative instincts began to race. Ben seemed anything but pleased with Karl's compliment. There was a lot of tension between the two men, and Nancy hoped she'd get a chance to question Ben—alone—to find out why.

Ben stared at Nancy for a moment, his dark blue eyes assessing her. "So you're the reporter," he said slowly. "You'll find a lot to write about here."

"All good, I hope," Karl quipped, giving Nancy another of his charming smiles.

"Of course." Ben made no attempt to hide his sarcasm.

"I'd like to interview you for the article, if that'd be okay with you," Nancy said to Ben.

After shooting Karl an icy look Ben told Nancy, "I'd be glad to tell you everything I know." The emphasis was on "everything," and Nancy felt her heart begin to beat faster.

"Can I arrange a private lesson?" Nancy asked. "We could do the interview on skis."

Ben shrugged. "I'm booked for the rest of the day. How about tomorrow morning? Nine o'clock?"

"Nine's fine," Nancy said.

At that moment the door to the school flew open and Jody Ashton rushed inside.

"Sorry I had to leave you," Jody said breathlessly, hurrying over to Nancy. "Are you ready for the rest of the tour?"

24

"I see you're back in good hands," Karl said to Nancy, "so I'll leave you. Don't forget, dinner tonight at eight."

When the door had closed behind Karl Ben raised an eyebrow at Nancy. "Aren't you lucky? Dinner with the great man." His lips curled in disgust.

"Mr. Reismueller has been very pleasant to me," Nancy said in her most professional manner.

"I'm sure he has," Ben shot back. "After all, you're a guest."

His words echoed what Jody had said, and Nancy had to wonder if a disgruntled employee could be responsible for the theft. Someone like Ben, for instance.

"I couldn't help overhearing your argument when I came in," Nancy said to Ben, taking out her notebook. "Why would you want to work for Rob Watson? The Tall Pines trails are a thousand times better than Rob's."

Ben flushed, glancing nervously at Nancy's notebook. "I was only joking," he said, pausing. "Rob doesn't have the kind of money Karl does. He wouldn't be able to pay me what I'm worth. But there would be one good thing about working at Watson's." Ben's blue eyes were serious as he met Nancy's. "Rob's not impressed with Scandinavian names like Inge."

"What do you mean?" Nancy asked, puzzled. She wondered if Ben was referring to Inge Gustafson—the name on the sign for the ski school. The name did seem familiar to her, but she couldn't place it.

Jody shifted from one foot to the other as though she were uncomfortable with the conversation. "Ben's just blowing off steam, aren't you, Ben?" she asked, giving him a warning look and changing the subject. "Don't you have a class?"

"Yeah," Ben replied, clamping his mouth shut. He stepped over to a row of lockers along one wall, opened one, and pulled out his ski clothes. His jacket bore the familiar Tall Pines insignia.

"What's going on?" Nancy asked Jody under her breath. "Who's Inge, and why is Ben so upset about her?"

Jody became even more uncomfortable. "It's no big deal," she told Nancy. "Karl hired Inge Gustafson, a Norwegian skier, to head the ski school."

Nancy nodded, realizing now why she'd thought she remembered the name. "I've heard of Inge. She's good." She had scanned a couple of back issues of *Tracks* to prepare for her cover, and one of the stories had been on Inge. "So what's the problem?"

"There *is* no problem," Jody insisted. "Inge's just delayed in coming over, and Ben's had to take on some of her work."

Nancy heard Ben slam his locker door. The ski instructor turned to face them. "Try *all* of her work," he said, and he headed out of the school.

Jody tried to smile brightly. "Ready to get fitted?" she asked, changing the subject.

"You bet," Nancy replied. She followed the girl

back through the entrance alcove and into the ski shop. Two walls of the shop were lined with new skis, boots, and poles, and a third was reserved for the rental area. A huge glass window filled the fourth wall. Nancy spotted Ben through it. His lesson had obviously started because he was in the middle of a group of skiers. There were a couple of other ski instructors outside, too, their Tall Pines logo jackets clearly visible. Ben skied over to talk to one of them for a moment.

Jody stepped over to a low counter next to the skis where a cashier stood. She came back with a tape measure. The girl worked quickly, writing down Nancy's height and shoe size and the length of poles she'd need. When she finished Jody said, "I'll make sure everything's ready for you tomorrow morning. Sorry I can't show you around anymore, but I have to get back to work."

"No problem," Nancy told her. "I think I'd like to rest a bit before dinner, anyway. Maybe take a sauna or check out that hot tub," she added with a grin.

"Good idea!" Jody said brightly. "See you later!" With a wave, she took off.

Nancy spied Ben taking his students off onto a trail and realized there was nothing more she could do for now. She yawned, realized that she really was a little tired, and decided to head back to her condo to unpack and rest before dinner. Bess and George should be arriving soon, she thought. Maybe she could find a way to talk to them before dinner.

* * *

Later Nancy had finished unpacking and was lying on her bed on top of the luxurious down comforter when the phone rang.

"Yes?" she answered in her most professional voice. "This is Nancy Drew."

"You mean the famous reporter from *Tracks*? You're my idol!" came George's familiar voice, laughing. "How's it going, Nan?"

"Fine, just fine." Nancy twirled the cord between her fingers.

"Have you learned anything yet?" George asked eagerly.

"No, but I have met Karl, Dave, Ben, and Jody."

George whistled over the phone line. "Wow! You were busy. Do you think any of them framed Rebecca?"

"I don't know," Nancy admitted. "Jody seems to hate her, but I don't know why yet." Nancy told George about Jody's reaction when she'd asked about Rebecca's being fired. "What's really interesting, though, is that Ben Wrobley has a major grudge against Tall Pines, and he talks as though he knows something shady's going on. I wonder if it's about the money."

George was silent for a moment. "Rebecca introduced me to Ben, and I skied with him once since the theft. But I never heard him say anything about it."

"Do you know why he's so unhappy at Tall Pines?" Nancy asked. "Why he resents Inge Gustafson so much?"

"Well, he's got good reason." George paused.

"Ben's a great skier and a terrific teacher, but what does he get for it?" She answered her own question. "Nothing. Inge gets all the credit and her name on the school, but she hasn't even shown up yet. Ben's doing his job and hers."

Nancy could understand why Ben was angry. The question was, was he angry enough to steal fifty thousand dollars? And why would he frame Rebecca for the theft? What could he have against her?

"Keep an eye on Ben, George," Nancy advised. "If you run into him, see what you can find out."

"Right," George said. "Hey, why don't we all meet in the sauna? Bess said she wanted to try it out."

"Great idea!" Nancy said. "But remember, if there's anyone else there, act like you don't know me."

"Nancy who? Who's ever heard of a Nancy Drew?" George joked, and she hung up.

Nancy laughed, got up, and quickly slipped into her parka and boots. On her way out she grabbed a gym bag, which already had her bathing suit and towel in it. The snow crunched under her feet as she made her way toward the fitness building. She was climbing the steps to the back entrance of the building when she was stopped by a familiar voice.

"Going to the pool?" Nancy turned to see Dave Kendall a few feet away. "I don't think it's open yet," he added.

She shook her head. "I'm trying the sauna."

Dave's smile was earnest. "I hope you're enjoying your stay so far."

"Oh, I am," Nancy assured him. "I wanted to ask you—"

Before she could finish her question Dave interrupted. "Why don't we schedule some time to talk? I'm sure you want to get into the sauna now." He stomped the snow off his boots. "How about tomorrow afternoon? Right after lunch?"

After Nancy nodded Dave waved and walked off. That's odd, Nancy thought as she watched him retreat. It was as if Dave hadn't wanted to talk to her.

Storing the thought away, Nancy entered the sauna and exercise area. There she was greeted by a friendly attendant wearing a forest green uniform. "I hope you enjoy our facilities," the attendant said as she handed Nancy a locker key and an oversize towel.

A minute later Bess and George joined Nancy in the locker room, and Nancy and Bess changed into their bathing suits while George put on sweats. George was going to work out and join them in the sauna afterward.

"This is a great place," Nancy said as she closed the door to the sauna and sat on a wooden bench.

"It sure is," Bess agreed. She leaned back against the wall and took a deep breath of the hot, dry air. "Wonderful," she murmured.

For a few minutes the girls relaxed in silence, letting the heat of the sauna work its magic.

Finally Bess opened her eyes and looked at

Nancy. "George told me you've been busy," she said.

Nancy laughed. "I guess I have. But not busy enough. I still don't know what Ben's so angry about, or why Jody hates Rebecca."

Bess was about to speak when they both heard someone at the door. Nancy held her finger to her lips, warning Bess to be quiet. She didn't want to get caught talking about the mystery. Bess nodded. When no one entered the sauna after a minute or two, Nancy shrugged.

"So what do we do next?" Bess asked, getting back to the case.

"We have to find out more about both Ben and Jody. You and George can help with that, because you're not pretending to be reporters. Jody's careful about what she says to me." Nancy leaned back against the wall. "I'm having dinner with the Reismuellers tonight. Why don't you and George come to my condo afterward, say around ten? We can work out a plan then."

Bess nodded and stood up. "I'm starting to feel cooked," she said, pulling her towel around her. "Let's go." She walked the three steps to the door and pushed on the handle.

"Nancy, the door won't open," Bess said, pushing on the handle again, surprise showing on her face.

"Push a little harder," Nancy suggested. "It's new. Maybe it just sticks."

Bess pushed. "Nancy, it doesn't work." This time her voice betrayed her mounting panic. "It's locked."

31

"That's strange," said Nancy, frowning. "Sauna doors don't have locks."

She came up beside Bess and tried the handle herself. The door wouldn't budge. She tried kicking the door. Still nothing.

Bess's face was flushed. "We've got to get out of here!" she cried. "I can't take this heat."

Nancy felt her own temperature rising, and she knew they couldn't stay much longer. Her eyes scanned the walls for a thermostat to turn the heat down. Nothing.

"The controls must be on the outside," she told Bess, trying to keep her voice calm.

"Oh, Nancy!" Bess wailed. "What are we going to do?"

Nancy pressed her face against the small window in the door and peered through it to the right and left. What she saw made her heart sink. Someone had wedged a piece of wood between the door and the frame.

They were locked in!

Chapter

Four

H ELP!" Bess shouted. "Somebody help!"

Nancy leaned against the door again and shoved, hoping to dislodge the wedge of wood. Nothing happened.

"We'll never get out of here!" Bess wailed.

"We'll get out, Bess," Nancy said with quiet determination. "There are lots of people around. Someone has to hear us shouting."

Bess gave Nancy a weak smile. "You're right," she said, wiping the sweat from her forehead. "I just hope that someone comes soon. I need to lose five pounds, not twenty," she joked. "Help!" she cried again, banging on the door.

At that moment Nancy heard footsteps outside the door and a loud scraping noise. Finally the door swung open.

"Thank goodness!" Bess flung herself out of the sauna and into the cooler air.

George was standing there, dressed in her sweats with a towel around her neck and a wedge-shaped piece of wood in her hand. "Why was this stuck in the door?" she asked, concern in her brown eyes.

"Someone barred the door," Nancy answered, shrugging her shoulders. She put an arm around Bess. "Maybe it was just a prank. Whoever did it must have known somebody would come along to let us out."

"I'm just glad it's over," Bess said. Nancy felt her friend start to shiver. "I'm ready to put on some clothes and grab a bite to eat. After that experience I need to rebuild my strength."

"I want to ask the attendant if she saw anything before I change," Nancy said. "And I'm going out to dinner tonight."

After Bess and George went into the locker room Nancy searched for the attendant. She found her sorting towels outside the locker room. As Nancy told her what happened the attendant became deathly white, and her eyes grew round.

"I left for only a minute. There were a lot of guests around," the girl told Nancy with a nervous shrug. "I'll keep my eyes open, though. That could have been dangerous!"

Nancy left her and went into the locker room to join Bess and George, but they had already gone. As Nancy changed she thought about the wedged door. Did the person who had done it want to trap her and Bess or someone else? Maybe it was just a prank played by someone who wanted to cause trouble at Tall Pines.

If the person was after Bess and Nancy, who knew they were going to be in the sauna? There was Jody, who had suggested it, and Dave Kendall, who saw her entering the building. Either one of them could have jammed the door. But why? It made no sense. As far as everyone at Tall Pines knew, Nancy was a reporter for *Tracks,* not a detective. Who would want to harm a reporter?

Unless . . . There was a possibility that her cover was blown and someone knew she was at Tall Pines investigating the theft. If so, Nancy could be in danger.

The air was cold with a hint of snow as Nancy headed back to her condo. It was seven-thirty; she'd barely have time to dress for dinner. She settled on a pair of black trousers and a teal blue silk blouse. A quick brush through her hair and a dash of pink lipstick and she was ready to go.

Nancy entered Edelweiss, just before eight. Crisp white linen cloths covered each table, and crystal glassware and silver flatware gleamed in the candlelight. Karl Reismueller greeted her just inside the door.

"Good evening," he said in a deep voice. "I'd like you to meet my wife, Sheila."

Sheila Reismueller was tall, thin, and stunning. She had dressed in a stylishly short rose-colored dress, and her champagne blond hair was swept up into a sophisticated French twist. Her hand was perched on her husband's arm, and Nancy thought the two of them made an elegant couple.

"I'm glad to meet you, Mrs. Reismueller,"

35

Nancy said. As she shook Sheila's hand Nancy noticed her perfume—roses and lilies with a hint of something spicy.

"Call me Sheila," the woman said, her blue eyes sparkling.

"And I insist you call me Karl. 'Mr. Reismueller' makes me feel a hundred years old."

The maître d' showed them to a table by the windows. When the women were seated he unfolded their napkins with a flourish.

"May I bring you an appetizer?" he asked.

Karl ordered fondue. "That's a fancy name for bread and melted cheese," he joked. "Where I'm from we always have it after a hard day's skiing."

"This is a gorgeous restaurant," Nancy said. Karl Reismueller's showmanship was obvious. Both the front and back walls of the restaurant were windowed. Several of the trails were lit, and the view was magnificent.

The waiter brought their fondue, and they set to dipping the toasted bread into the steaming pot of melted cheese. Nancy remarked on the vases of fresh roses on each table. "The flowers are wonderful," she said.

"You can thank Sheila for them," Karl said with a fond glance at his wife. "She insists that we have fresh flowers every night."

"It might seem to be an extravagance, but I just love fresh flowers," Sheila said. "That's why we named the restaurant Edelweiss."

Nancy remembered the orchids in Dave

Kendall's office and asked Sheila if she was responsible for them, too.

"No," she said, laughing lightly and fingering a large horseshoe-shaped pin on her left shoulder. Nancy assumed those were real diamonds covering the pin's surface.

"Dave deserves the compliments," Sheila said. "Indoor gardening is one of his hobbies, and, as you saw, he's awfully good at it."

"Dave's also a good manager," Karl added as the waiter cleared the fondue pot from their table. "He's responsible for whatever success we're having." Nancy noticed Bess and George taking seats at the table next to them.

Sheila turned to Nancy. "My husband is too modest," she said. "He's the genius behind this and our other businesses. Why, his printing company is the biggest in the state, and his chain of toy stores just keeps growing." She laid her hand on his arm. "Isn't that right, Karl?"

Karl frowned slightly. "Let's not bore Nancy, Sheila," he said. "Tell me, have you had a chance to ski any of the trails?"

Nancy shook her head. "I'm skiing with Ben at nine tomorrow morning, though."

"You and Sheila ought to ski together," Karl said. "She knows the trails as well as any instructor at Tall Pines."

"I'd like that," Nancy agreed.

"It'll have to be the day after tomorrow," Sheila told Karl. "I have several appointments tomorrow."

Taking a sip of water, Nancy turned to Karl. She decided it was time to get whatever information she could on the theft. "I heard about the theft you had here," she said. "I understand the police weren't able to recover most of the money."

Sheila's face grew pale. "That was the last thing we needed, more money prob—"

"We feel we know who took the money," Karl interrupted smoothly, "but have decided not to press charges. The publicity would be far too damaging. I certainly hope," he added with a rueful smile, "that nothing about that unfortunate incident will end up in the pages of *Tracks.*"

Nancy smiled and offered a quiet no. She did wonder whether Sheila had started to say "money problems." She hadn't heard of any at Tall Pines.

Before Nancy could ask any more questions, Karl moved on to the subject of Tall Pines's other attractions. As they ate their filet mignon followed by baked Alaska and coffee he amused them with anecdotes about the resort and its opening.

"Thank you for a lovely meal," Nancy said as they were leaving. "The Edelweiss will get a great write-up in our magazine."

Karl smiled, his white teeth glistening in the candlelight. "Now, that's what I like to hear!" he said. "Come, Sheila." He pulled back his wife's chair and took her arm. "This has been a long day. Come see me tomorrow, Nancy, if you like. You know where to find me."

38

Nancy waited for the elegant couple to leave the dining room before motioning to Bess and George, who were still sitting at the table next to hers. "See you at my condo in ten minutes," she whispered softly as she passed by them.

The three friends were in the living room of Nancy's condo, and she was just finishing telling them what she thought Sheila Reismueller was going to say before her husband had cut her off.

George had built a small fire while Nancy talked, and Bess was curled up in one of the oversize chairs.

"I don't see how it fits into the case," Nancy admitted, "but I want to check it out."

A frown crossed George's face. "We're here to clear Rebecca," she reminded Nancy.

Nancy nodded. She had a plan ready. "I want to follow up with Ben. I need to find out what kind of shady things he thinks are going on here, so I've scheduled a lesson with him tomorrow morning." She turned to Bess. "Would you cover Jody? Find out if there's any reason she needs money. And also find out why she seems to hate Rebecca so much."

Bess grinned. "No problem. I wanted to check out the ski shop anyway."

George raised a questioning eyebrow. "What should I do?"

Nancy thought for a moment. "Why don't you go over to Rob Watson's lodge tomorrow and see what you can find out there?" Nancy continued explaining. "Tall Pines is Rob's biggest rival. He may be trying to sabotage the resort."

"It's a real sacrifice, you know, leaving Tall Pines to go to Rob's," George said with a laugh.

"Let's meet here again tomorrow night," Nancy suggested as the girls were leaving.

Nancy stood in the doorway and watched them walk off toward the main lodge, where they were staying. Snow had started to fall lightly. As she went back inside she decided to check out Dave Kendall's office, where the theft had occurred.

Three whole weeks had passed, and Nancy knew she was probably wasting her time but felt a need to check it out anyway. She grabbed her ski parka and within a few minutes was at the Tall Pines administration building. Making sure no one was around, Nancy gently shoved against the front door. She was surprised that it was open.

Also surprising was the light streaming out from under Dave's office door. Someone was in there.

Nancy decided that at that time of night it was probably a cleaning crew. Then she heard someone speak and recognized the man's voice as Dave's. She was wrong—Dave was working late. As she was planning her next move the outside door to the building was flung open, and a blast of cold air rushed in. Nancy turned, wondering who was coming into the office so late.

A short, stocky man in black ski clothes stomped snow from his feet, then stopped as soon as he noticed Nancy. For an instant neither of them spoke. Nancy's eyes widened in recognition. It was Rob Watson! She'd seen his photograph in a back issue of *Tracks,* and the ruddy face, bright blue eyes, and long, curly white hair were unmistakable.

"What are you doing here?" Nancy demanded.

The man swiveled his head from Nancy to the door behind him.

"What's going on?" Nancy asked again.

Before Nancy could stop him Watson spun around and raced out the door.

Chapter

Five

WHAT WAS Rob Watson doing sneaking around Tall Pines at night? Nancy wondered, running to the door.

"What's going on?"

Nancy was stopped by Dave Kendall calling to her from the open doorway of his office. "What are you doing here?" he demanded brusquely.

Nancy ignored his question. "Rob Watson was here a minute ago, but when he saw me he ran out," she explained.

"Watson?" Dave grimaced. "What was he doing here?"

"I don't know," Nancy replied, shrugging her shoulders. "Maybe he came to check out his competition."

Rob's appearance at Tall Pines was definitely strange, and Nancy couldn't help wondering whether it was connected to the theft. She doubted Rob would have stolen the money himself but thought he could be working with a Tall Pines employee.

Kendall brushed off the question with a shake of his head. "I doubt it." Then he paused and studied her curiously. "Is there a reason *you're* here so late?" he asked Nancy.

"Actually, th-there is," Nancy stammered, searching for an excuse. The last thing she wanted was for Dave to think she was snooping around his office. She quickly explained about the accident in the sauna.

"I'm sorry that happened to you," Dave said, showing obvious concern. "I'll tell the attendant to be on guard." Nancy thought she heard Dave mumble something about "not again."

"What was that?" she asked.

Dave looked at her carefully, squinting his eyes. "I don't want this to be published—"

"Off the record," Nancy assured him.

"We have a prankster here at Tall Pines," Dave confessed. "Nothing serious, but this isn't our first incident. I was just dictating a short memo to Karl about it."

He opened his mouth as though he was going to say something more but stopped instead and took a breath. When he spoke again his words were measured. "I hope you understand that none of this is to get around," he said. "If Karl finds out I told you, he'll fire me."

Nancy nodded. Though she might need to tell Karl about the blocked sauna door, she had no reason to divulge Dave's confidence. Maybe he was right. Maybe it had just been a prank and not meant specifically for her and Bess.

Before nine the next morning Nancy met Jody at the rental office to pick up her skis, boots, and poles.

"I wish the new equipment had come in," Jody said when she handed Nancy her gear. "You'd go crazy over the new boots and bindings. They're state-of-the-art material. Really lightweight. Plus the boots go up over your ankles, which offers extra support."

"I've heard about them at *Tracks*," Nancy fibbed. "I've been dying to try them."

"We're expecting a shipment any day," Jody told her. "With a little luck it'll arrive before you leave, and I'll make sure you get a set."

"Morning, Ben," Nancy said, spotting the instructor in the entrance alcove. "Ready for my lesson?"

Ben smiled and pushed a lock of his jet-black hair off his forehead. "You bet," he said.

Picking up her skis and poles, Nancy followed him outside to the trail head. A small crowd of guests had gathered by the trail map. Ben greeted several people by name before hooking his boots into the bindings. Nancy noticed that he had new bindings, and his boots were higher than hers.

"Ready?" Ben asked.

"Don't expect a lot," Nancy said as she slipped her hands into the pole straps. "This is my first time out this season." She looked down at her clothes. She was wearing a cherry-red outfit. "When I first learned to ski we wore jeans and parkas. Now it's neon speed suits and high-tech equipment."

Ben chuckled and led the way to what he said was one of the most popular trails. "I like to ski this one before it's crowded."

Though a light snow had fallen overnight, the tracks, which had been set the previous day, were still visible. As Ben gracefully skied into the left pair of tracks Nancy placed her skis in the right ones. "Not all our trails have two sets of tracks," Ben explained, "but it's easier to teach on them."

Nancy was a little nervous that Ben might notice she hadn't skied in a while. A reporter for a ski magazine should look pretty good on the trails. Although it took her a few glides to get used to her new equipment, Nancy was soon moving at a pretty good pace. "These skis are great!" she exclaimed, noticing that they glided farther than any she'd tried before.

They skied until they were deep in the forest. "You're good at the diagonal stride," Ben said, referring to the basic cross-country kick and glide. He tugged his zipper pull up, and Nancy noticed that hooked to it was a small thermometer. "The conditions are just about perfect. Do you want to learn to skate?"

Nancy was confused. "I thought this was a skiing lesson."

"I wasn't talking about ice skating. This is ski skating." While Nancy watched he took his left ski out of the track and pushed forward with it and his poles. A second later, he was gliding gracefully along the trail on his right ski.

"Wow!" Nancy said when Ben turned and whooshed to a stop in front of her. "That looks like fun."

"It is," he assured her. "Now watch. Your left ski is the skate ski. You push with that one and glide on the other. The trick is all in shifting your weight."

"You make it look easy."

Ben grinned. "It is—once you learn how."

As she practiced the new technique Nancy realized what a good instructor Ben was. Not only was he an expert skier, but he knew how to explain the movements. At the end of a few minutes Nancy felt confident trying to skate.

When they reached a hill Ben suggested she use a herringbone step to climb it.

"I didn't know there were hills around here," she said as she put her skis in the V position. Instead of gliding she stepped up the incline, keeping the tips of her skis far apart while the tails remained close together to prevent her from sliding backward.

"There weren't any hills until a few months ago," Ben told her. "Karl brought in bulldozers to contour slopes. He wants Tall Pines to be the perfect resort."

"But that's impossible, isn't it?" Nancy asked. This was the opening she needed. "For example, I heard you had a robbery here."

Nancy could feel Ben's eyes on her. When he

finally did reply, his voice was cold. "It's nothing for you to worry about. I know you reporters like sensationalism, but you don't have to put that in your article."

"We heard about it around the office," she pressed, ignoring his comment. "Why do you suppose that girl took the money?"

They had stopped moving and were standing side by side now. Ben's anger was apparent to Nancy. "Did you come here to ski or to ask questions about Rebecca Montgomery?"

He sounded almost hostile now, and Nancy sensed she'd touched a nerve. He certainly hadn't minded bad-mouthing the resort the day before. She didn't know why Ben wouldn't want to talk about Rebecca now, unless he knew something about the theft.

She shrugged. "News is news," she said. "For example, it might be news to our readers that I heard you talking to both Dave and Karl yesterday, and it was pretty obvious that you felt something's very wrong at Tall Pines."

Ben studied Nancy for a long time. "Nothing's wrong," he said. "Nothing a ski reporter would be interested in," he added for emphasis.

Nancy wondered whether Karl had spoken to Ben, warning him not to talk to her. "Come on, Ben," she said. "I don't believe that."

He shrugged. "It's true," he declared. "Now if you don't mind, I'd like to ski." The finality in Ben's voice told Nancy that she'd learn nothing more from him that morning.

They made their way back to the school in

silence. As they approached the end of the trail, Nancy said, "I may want another lesson. When do you teach?" What Nancy really wanted to know was Ben's schedule, and if he could have locked her and Bess in the sauna.

Ben smiled. "I'm pretty busy. We'd have to schedule a lesson early if you want to go out again." He glanced at his watch. "To tell you the truth, Nancy, I don't think you need another lesson. You're good."

Nancy laughed. "Thanks. I may need some pointers, though, because I want to try all the trails before I leave."

They skied to a stop, and Nancy released her bindings. "Are you Ben?" she heard a familiar voice ask. It was Bess, dressed in new ski clothes and carrying skis and poles over one shoulder. There was no risk of losing Bess in the woods, Nancy thought with a smile, not with her neon pink pants and green and orange jacket!

"Can you point me to a novice trail?" Bess asked Ben.

He gave her an appraising glance. "Do you have a partner? If you're a beginner, you shouldn't ski alone."

Bess shrugged. "My cousin deserted me for the day."

Turning to Nancy, Ben suggested, "Why don't you go with her? You said you wanted the practice."

"Sure," Nancy said. Skiing with Bess would give her a chance to find out if her friend had learned anything from Jody. She gave Bess a knowing look. "I'm always happy to have a ski partner. I'm Nancy Drew," she said, holding out her gloved hand.

"Bess Marvin," Bess said.

"Can you suggest a quiet trail?" Nancy turned to ask Ben.

He pulled a trail map out of his pocket. "Take Aerie," he said, showing Nancy the route. "You'll see a small hut here, and another trail branches off it." He pointed to the trail junction. "Be careful not to go on that one. You'd be able to handle it, but Cascades is too difficult for a beginner."

Nancy thanked Ben. "No problem," he said. Just then Jody came out of the shop and school entrance and pulled Ben aside. "Excuse us," Jody said, smiling at Nancy.

"Ready?" Nancy asked Bess, who had been putting her skis on with Nancy.

Bess nodded, and the two of them skied over to where the track began. Once they were safely out of sight Nancy asked Bess, "Did you have a chance to talk to Jody?"

"Not very much," she said. "There were a lot of customers when I went in so we made a date to meet for lunch." Bess reached forward with one pole and pushed off.

"You're doing well," Nancy said, skiing up next to Bess. Her eyes were on her friend, but her mind was on the mystery. She was scheduled to be at Tall Pines for only a week, so that gave her six more days to find the thief. Not a lot of time.

"Cross country's not as hard as I expected,

and the clothes are fun," Bess said, interrupting Nancy's thoughts.

When they reached the small hut Ben had mentioned Nancy stopped. "Check out the view," she said. Though it seemed that they'd climbed only a small distance, the forest ended right where they stood, and there was a drop in front of them.

"It's pretty," Bess agreed as she cautiously slid her skis backward. "I don't like the cliff, though. Let's go. It makes me feel dizzy."

Nancy looked at the trail signs: Cascade veered off to the right, Aerie to the left. The girls skied left.

"Whew!" Bess said a few minutes later. She was out of breath from climbing a small hill. "This is getting harder."

Nancy had to admit that Bess was right. For a novice trail, Aerie was very difficult. As they continued the trail grew narrower, and the second set of tracks ended. Instead of leveling out the trail continued to climb. Nancy slid her skis into the tracks behind Bess, calling out encouragement. "Just a little farther," she said, urging Bess to try the herringbone step.

When they reached the top of the incline Bess raised her poles in triumph. "I made it," she said, and her skis inched forward.

Before Bess could get her poles down and steady herself she was sliding quickly down the back side of the steep hill. Nancy gasped. The trail made a sharp right turn ahead, just before a skier would fly directly into a stream.

"Bess!" Nancy called.

It was too late. Bess was already careening down the trail, her arms and poles windmilling, headed straight for the rocky stream.

"Help!" Nancy heard Bess cry out. "Help me, Nancy! I can't stop!"

Chapter

Six

NANCY WATCHED in horror as Bess flailed her arms, trying to get a grip in the snow with her poles. At the rate Bess was going she would soon land headfirst in the icy stream. Nancy's mind raced for a solution.

"Let yourself fall, Bess!" Nancy shouted at her friend.

Bess chose not to or couldn't make herself fall. Instead she dragged her poles, trying to slow herself down. She was less than fifty feet from the stream.

Nancy knew she had to do something. Jabbing her poles in the snow, she hurled herself forward behind Bess.

The slope was incredibly steep, but Nancy managed to keep her balance and gain on Bess. Finally, when Nancy was right behind her friend, she reached out and grabbed the back of Bess's jacket and yanked—hard. The two girls fell, tumbling to the ground. When they came to a halt, Nancy saw the cold, rocky stream less than ten feet in front of them.

"That was close!" Bess said, breathing heavily. "If you hadn't pulled me down—" She stopped, and her eyes grew large with fear.

"Don't think about it," Nancy urged. She stood up on her skis and gave Bess a hand up. "Come on. I think we've had enough skiing for today."

Slowly Nancy and Bess made their way down the rest of the trail toward the head area. All the while Nancy tried to figure out what had happened. The trail she and Bess had ended up on was obviously not for novices. That meant that Ben had given them the wrong directions, or someone had switched the markers. Either way, she and Bess had been in danger.

"George!" Nancy heard Bess cry out when they finally made their way back to the trail head. "Oh, George, you'll never believe what just happened."

Nancy was surprised to see George at Tall Pines. She was supposed to have gone to Watson's for the day.

When Bess told her cousin what had happened, George let out a low whistle. "Sounds like more trouble for Tall Pines," she said.

Nancy nodded her agreement. Making sure that no one was around to overhear their conversation, Nancy said, "I want to check out what just happened. Do you have a trail map?"

George pulled one out of her jacket pocket and opened it up. "Here's where Aerie meets Cascade." Her fingers traced the trails back to the trail head. "I see how to get back there. Can you get back to the room by yourself, Bess?"

"Sure," Bess said. "It's time for my lunch date anyway," she said. Nancy and George waved and skied off. After a few minutes they were heading up Aerie. "What do you think happened, Nan?" George asked when they were alone.

Nancy slowed her pace. "I don't know, but I don't think it was an accident," she told George. "Especially after what happened in the sauna. Either Bess and I wandered into a trap set for somebody else, or someone's after me or Bess."

"But why?" George asked, panting slightly as they made an uphill climb.

"I'm beginning to wonder if my cover's been blown," Nancy said. "Maybe someone knows I'm a detective and wants to scare me off."

"Don't jump to conclusions," George warned. "You've always told me that's a sign of bad detective work."

Nancy laughed. "Okay. You're right. But what other reason could there be?"

"First we have to find out if the signs were switched, then who switched them. Then we'll have our reason for why the person did it," George said, pleased with herself.

Nancy was quiet as they took a slow downhill glide. At a flat part in the trail she stopped and said, "Ben knew where we were going. He could have told Jody, too. I saw them talking together before Bess and I skied off."

"Ben seems to admire Rob Watson. What if they're working together to cause trouble at Tall Pines?" George asked. Then she shook her head. "What am I saying? He's too nice a guy to do anything like that."

"Hey," Nancy said, stopping short. "I nearly forgot. Did you go to Watson's this morning?"

"You bet I did," George replied. "I almost didn't recognize the place. Major construction. They're expanding the snack bar and upgrading the trails."

"It sounds like Rob's spending a lot of money," Nancy said.

"That's what I thought," George agreed. "He could have gotten a bank loan, or—"

"He could be behind the Tall Pines theft," Nancy finished. Nancy and George climbed the incline to the hut that marked the point where Aerie met Cascades. "Let's stop here," Nancy said. "I want to check something." She pulled George's trail map from her pocket to study it. It confirmed what she had guessed.

"According to the map, Aerie turns right, but the sign is pointing left." Someone had switched "Aerie" with "Cascades." Nancy carefully turned the signs so they pointed to the right trails.

"I can't believe Ben would do something like that," George said, frowning. "It must have been someone else."

Nancy didn't say anything. As George was speaking, she noticed something glinting in the snow. She bent closer, picked up the object, and whistled softly. It was a thermometer just like the one she'd seen attached to Ben's zipper. Silently she handed the tiny thermometer over to her friend.

George's expression was serious. "It does look like Ben's thermometer," she said, her voice a bit defensive. "But I'm sure there's a logical explanation. Ben wouldn't try to hurt you or anyone. Also, when would he have done it?"

Nancy put the thermometer in her pocket. "I hope you're right" was all she said.

The girls skied silently for several minutes, moving across a snow-covered meadow. The real Aerie trail skirted the edge of the man-made hill and went through a meadow rather than through the forest.

"That must be the ice-skating pond," George said as they approached a large open area. A half-finished building stood at the far end of the secluded frozen pond. Construction tape surrounded the pond to keep people out. Nancy remembered that the outdoor rink wasn't ready for guests yet.

As the girls skied past the ice two people emerged from the building being constructed. Nancy recognized the tall, slender woman in the shocking pink ski outfit as Sheila Reismueller. The man was a stranger. Seeing the furtive way that Sheila glanced around, Nancy quickly pulled George behind a bushy evergreen so Sheila wouldn't see them.

"He doesn't look like the normal Tall Pines visitor, does he?" George asked in a whisper. Instead of fashionable ski wear, the man was dressed in a black and white houndstooth suit, a black felt fedora, and an overcoat tossed casually over his shoulders. He would have looked more at home on a city street than at a ski resort.

Nancy nodded. "And Sheila looks like she doesn't want to be seen."

"I wonder what's going on," George murmured.

"Maybe he's a contractor," Nancy suggested, shaking herself. "I'm probably being paranoid because of the case." Perhaps Karl had asked Sheila to help with something, and that was why she hadn't gone to do her errands that day as she'd planned.

A few minutes later the girls resumed skiing and slid to a graceful stop at the end of the trail.

"I'm going to get some lunch," George said. "Want to join me?"

Nancy shook her head. "I have an apple to eat. Then I have an appointment to talk to Dave Kendall," she said. "Why don't you track Ben after your lunch? See what he's up to."

"No problem," George said. "He's the best instructor here. I wouldn't mind following him," she added with a smile. "Nancy, I really don't think Ben's involved, but if you want me to keep an eye on him, I will."

"Thanks, George," Nancy said. "If you see her, would you tell Bess to meet me at the pool at three? I want to find out if she got anything out of Jody."

"You got it," George said. With that, she skied off toward the Tall Pines ski school.

After removing her skis Nancy dropped them off at the rental counter and made her way to Dave Kendall's office. Even if he'd taken a late lunch, she thought, he should be back in his office by now.

The receptionist was away from her desk, but the door to Dave's office was open a bit, so Nancy walked to the door and started to call to him. She stopped herself as soon as she realized the man in the office was not Dave Kendall.

Intrigued, Nancy remained at the door, peering in. She watched as the man slid some papers off Dave's desk and into his backpack. A moment later he picked up the backpack and turned around, holding it in front of him.

It was Ben Wrobley!

Nancy pushed the door open and stepped inside. "Well, hello, Ben," Nancy said innocently.

"Nancy! What are you doing here?" There was no mistaking the nervous quaver in Ben's voice. It was obvious to Nancy that Ben hadn't wanted to get caught in Dave's office. What was the ski instructor up to? She was dying to ask him but knew it would totally blow her cover if she did.

"I wanted to interview Dave this afternoon," she said instead. "Is he around?"

Ben gestured toward the empty office. "Dave was called away."

"That's weird," Nancy said, making a face. "He asked me to meet with him this afternoon."

"It was an unexpected trip, he said." Ben smiled—a little too brightly, in Nancy's opinion. "Maybe he left a message for you with the receptionist." Ben must have noticed Nancy staring at his backpack because he mumbled, "Karl asked me to pick up a couple things from Dave's office for him."

Ben might be telling the truth, Nancy thought, but that didn't explain his nervousness when he had first seen her. Besides, after the scene she'd witnessed the day before in the ski shop, Nancy doubted that Karl would ask Ben to help him.

Ben took another step toward the door. "Dave won't be back for another hour," he told Nancy. It was obvious that he badly wanted to get out of Dave's office, but Nancy wasn't going to let him leave so soon. First there was something she had to check out. She moved forward quickly and pretended to stumble. Ben dropped his pack to help her steady herself. Nancy's eyes moved quickly to the front of his parka.

The thermometer that had been on Ben Wrobley's zipper pull was gone.

Chapter

Seven

I HAVE SOMETHING of yours," Nancy said. Reaching into her pocket, she pulled out the thermometer and held it out to him.

Ben's face broke into a smile. "Thanks!" he said, taking it. "Where'd you find it?"

"Right where the Aerie and Cascades trails meet," she said, watching Ben's expression.

He shrugged, obviously unaware of the significance of what she had just said. "It must have fallen off this morning," he told her.

"Oh, really," Nancy said. "I remember that you looked at the temperature when we were out."

Ben nodded as he clipped the thermometer back onto his jacket. "True. I must have lost it afterward. My ten o'clock student canceled, so I tried to find you and Bess up by the hut where the trails meet. I guess it fell off then."

Ben's explanation sounded plausible, but Nancy still wasn't convinced. "Did you notice that the trail signs were switched?" she asked.

"What?" Ben's blue eyes widened in surprise. "That could have been dangerous."

"You bet," Nancy agreed. "The girl I was skiing with could hardly get down the trail."

Ben seemed to be outraged. "I'm going to straighten this out. We can't risk anyone getting hurt." His concern seemed genuine. Maybe George was right, and Ben wouldn't hurt anyone. But that didn't explain what he'd put into his backpack or why he'd been so secretive.

Ben zipped his jacket closed and slipped into the straps of his backpack. "Thanks for telling me about the trail signs being switched. I've got a class now, but afterward I'm going out to check *all* the signs."

With that Ben left, taking whatever papers he had stuffed into his backpack with him. Nancy was frustrated that she couldn't ask him any more questions about what he was doing in Dave's office, but the last thing she wanted was to blow her cover—especially with him. He was still a prime suspect as far as she was concerned.

Ben had given her one important fact: Dave wouldn't be back for almost an hour. That gave Nancy the chance to search his office.

Nancy scanned the office and decided that searching the files and desk drawers would be the best way to begin.

She sat down at Rebecca's desk and methodically went through each of the drawers. Nothing. Dave's desk was next. The top two drawers contained only routine business papers. Nancy started to leaf through the folders in the lower file drawer and found one labeled Rob Watson.

She pulled it out and began to read. The folder contained a confidential report about Rob's ski camp. Was this folder why Rob had come into the office building the night before?

Nancy guessed Karl had ordered the report before he built Tall Pines because he'd wanted to know what his competition was. According to the report, Rob's profits were minimal. So how could he afford the major construction George had seen?

Nancy glanced at her watch. Dave should be back in about ten minutes, and she didn't want him to find her in his office. She moved to the row of file cabinets and leafed through them quickly. Nothing unusual. There was a drawer of personnel files and one devoted to the building permits the county and state required.

Nancy was about to leaf through the personnel files when she heard a noise in the outer office. Quickly she closed the file drawer and made her way to the door. Outside she heard the receptionist singing. As casually as possible, Nancy closed the door to Dave's office and walked toward the reception area.

"I'm Nancy Drew," she told the receptionist,

a petite woman with curly black hair. "I had an appointment with Mr. Kendall and was waiting for him in his office, but he hasn't shown up."

"Mr. Kendall just called. He's still out of town," the receptionist informed her.

Nancy checked her watch. It was nearly three, and she wanted to meet Bess at the pool. "Could you please tell Mr. Kendall that I couldn't wait for him? I'll contact him myself to reschedule our appointment."

The receptionist smiled and wrote down the message. "Of course, Ms. Drew."

Ten minutes later Nancy and Bess were lying on lounge chairs by the side of the pool. Although there were a dozen people in the pool, no one was in the area Bess had chosen. They'd be able to talk without being overheard.

"Did you have lunch with Jody?" Nancy asked.

"She didn't show. I waited for fifteen minutes. Then I went to the shop. Jody told me she'd been even more swamped after I left this morning and couldn't get away." Bess's expression became serious. "Nancy, she was lying about part of that time."

Nancy raised an eyebrow. "What makes you think that?" she asked under her breath.

"A customer came in while I was there. She was complaining about the shop having been closed this morning."

"When was that?" Maybe Jody had had

the opportunity to switch the trail signs after all.

"The customer was loud and clear about the time. She told Jody three times that the shop had been closed between ten-fifteen and ten forty-five."

The timing was right. Jody would have had long enough to ski to the warming hut, switch the signs, and come back.

"I don't like the sound of that," Nancy said.

Bess sat up and smiled at a boy who'd just climbed out of the pool. "Are you going to talk to Jody?"

Nancy nodded. "I think I'll invite her to have dinner with me tonight."

"I'm so glad you could make it," Nancy said as she and Jody met at the entrance to Edelweiss. The maître d' showed them to a table for four, then pulled out their chairs.

"You don't think I'd pass up an opportunity to eat here, do you?" Jody asked. "I can't begin to afford it."

The girls opened their menus. "The Creole chicken sounds great," Jody said. "I love spicy food."

"I think I'll have the broiled salmon. Be sure to save room for dessert," she said, glancing around the room. George and Bess were seated in one corner—with Ben. On the opposite side of the room Dave was sitting with Sheila and Karl Reismueller.

"I knew Sheila would wear something white

tonight," Jody said. When Nancy appeared puzzled, Jody touched the small crystal vase filled with lilies of the valley. "Sheila has two special habits. She always wears her diamond horseshoe pin, and her dinner clothes always match the flowers."

The waiter appeared at their table. "Are you ready to order?" he asked. Nancy selected French onion soup followed by broiled salmon, while Jody chose shrimp cocktail and the Creole chicken.

"I'm starved," Jody said. "I never got a real lunch break."

Here was Nancy's opening. "I heard the shop was closed for a while this morning," she commented. "Someone said you took an early lunch." Or maybe you made a quick trip to switch some trail signs, Nancy added silently.

For a second Jody seemed surprised. "I had a family emergency," she said. "My mother locked her keys in her car, so I had to race into Monroe to rescue her. She was an hour late for work already, and I really had to help her."

"That's too bad," Nancy said, making a mental note to check Jody's alibi. She reached for her purse and pulled out her reporter's notebook. "I'd like a little background info for my article, if you don't mind."

Jody smiled, but she seemed nervous. Her unease made Nancy wonder if Jody had something to hide.

"Where did you work before Tall Pines?" Nancy asked.

"Jensen's department store during the day," Jody answered. "At night I was a short-order cook at the Arch Diner."

"Two jobs, wow! You must have been tired all the time."

Jody shrugged. "I'm saving money for college," she explained as the waiter placed a crock of steaming soup in front of Nancy and shrimp on a bed of ice in front of Jody.

Nancy took a spoonful of the soup. "This is delicious," she said, and cut through the melted cheese to taste the savory onion and beef broth below.

"Good evening, ladies," Nancy heard Karl Reismueller say in his faintly accented voice. She looked up to see him, Sheila, and Dave standing next to the table.

"I hope you're enjoying your dinner," Karl continued. He reached out to shake Nancy's hand as she and Jody rose to greet the three older people.

"It's delicious," Nancy assured him. She smiled at Sheila, and her eyes moved over the front of the dress, searching for her trademark pin. How odd, she thought. Sheila wasn't wearing the diamond horseshoe.

As Karl discussed business with Jody, Dave turned to Nancy. "Sorry I didn't make it back for our interview this afternoon. Why don't you stop by tomorrow at about eleven?"

Nancy agreed. She glanced over his shoulder

toward the back of the room and saw that George, Bess, and Ben were leaving their table.

"Ben!" Karl called as the threesome approached. "I hope you gave Nancy a good lesson this morning."

Ben's expression was wary, and Nancy guessed he was remembering their last conversation. "I tried my best," he said.

George and Bess started talking to Jody while Karl said something to Ben in a low voice.

"We never did plan our skiing for tomorrow," Sheila said to Nancy. She gestured toward the window where a group of skiers had emerged from the forested trails. "Perhaps you'd like to go this evening. Night skiing is great fun."

Though Nancy had planned to spend the rest of the evening reviewing the case with George and Bess, she quickly agreed. She could meet the girls later.

George moved to Nancy's side. "We'll go to the movies," she whispered so that no one else could hear. "Then we'll meet you at your condo when we get back—around ten, okay?"

Nancy nodded her head slightly.

"Be careful!" Dave said as Nancy felt the table jolt in front of her.

"Sorry." Ben's face flushed red—he was obviously embarrassed. "Someone bumped into me. I didn't mean to crash into the table."

Sheila turned quickly. "Is everything all right?" she asked.

Nancy noticed a small wet stain on the otherwise spotless tablecloth. "Something spilled," she said. Then she saw that the flower vase was lying on its side. "The flowers tipped over."

"I'll have the waiter bring more water," Sheila said. Dave straightened the vase, and Sheila rearranged the lilies of the valley. Sheila then put her hand on Karl's arm. "We'd better leave Nancy and Jody to enjoy their food while it's still hot," she said.

Bess winked as she, George, and Ben took off. The Reismuellers and Dave excused themselves, leaving Nancy and Jody to eat their dinners. Nancy took another spoonful of soup. The thick crust of cheese was disturbed only in one spot, so the soup had been kept warm. It was now a perfect temperature.

"Gosh, it was almost like we had a Tall Pines staff meeting," Jody said with a grin, and she speared a shrimp.

"It was crowded all of a sudden," Nancy agreed.

After she took another spoonful of soup Nancy heard Jody's voice as if from a distance. "Are you all right, Nancy?" the girl was saying.

Nancy felt her face grow hot. A wave of dizziness passed over her. "I'm fine," she managed to say. "It's awfully hot in here, though, don't you think?"

Jody was staring at her as if she was concerned. "Not really. Are you sure you're okay?"

Nancy was about to answer her when she felt a sharp stabbing sensation grip her stomach.

It hurt so much, she doubled over from the pain.

"Nancy!" Jody cried, leaning toward her. "What's wrong?"

She tried to force out an answer, but the pain was too intense. The last thing she remembered was tumbling to the floor. Then everything went black.

Chapter

Eight

Nancy opened her eyes. Where was she? Her head was killing her, and her stomach was tied in knots. Looking up at tablecloths and chairs, she realized that she was lying on her back on the floor of the Edelweiss. Jody was kneeling next to her. Nancy pulled herself up slowly, wincing at the pain.

"What happened?" Nancy asked.

"I don't know." Jody's pale face and worried expression told Nancy something terrible had happened. "One second we were talking, and the next you just keeled over and passed out. I called a doctor. Thank goodness there's always one on call for ski accidents."

Though her legs were still shaky, with Jody and the maître d's help Nancy was able to walk to the small employees' lounge off the kitchen. "You'd better lie down," Jody advised, pointing to a couch.

Nancy closed her eyes again, hoping the pain in her stomach would go away—fast. A few minutes later she heard the door open.

"I'm Dr. Gorman," a gray-haired man said, slipping a stethoscope around his neck. "What happened?"

Nancy shook her head. "I'm not sure. I passed out. But right before I did, I had terrible pains. It still hurts," she added, holding her hands to her stomach.

"It must be food poisoning," Jody said.

The doctor asked Jody to leave while he examined Nancy. "What did you eat?" he asked as he took her blood pressure.

"Just French onion soup. It tasted fine."

"Hmm." Dr. Gorman slid a thermometer under Nancy's tongue and checked her pulse. "I don't think it's food poisoning," he told her. "Usually you don't see symptoms of that until three to four hours after eating."

He was silent for a moment as he filled a needle with a clear serum. "Your pulse is still quite slow," he said, giving her an injection.

"If it's not food poisoning . . ." Nancy began, looking expectantly at Dr. Gorman.

The doctor hesitated a moment, then finished packing up his kit. "It could be several things, including a virus. Just to be sure, I'm sending your soup to a lab to be tested. When I get the results I'll let you know. You should be fine now, but you must go straight to bed. Do you need help getting to your room?"

Jody came in and said she'd help Nancy, and the doctor left. "You'll be okay?" Jody asked when they got to Nancy's front door.

Nancy assured Jody that she was fine. "I'll go straight to bed," she said. "My stomach needs all the rest it can get."

Jody laughed a little, then her sparkling green eyes grew serious. "I'm going to tell Mr. Reismueller about this. I tried to find him and his wife when the doctor got there, but they'd left. I'll call him right now, though. He should know. The negative publicity—"

Nancy stopped her short. "My meal at the Edelweiss last night was perfect and earned a rave review. The doctor wasn't convinced I had food poisoning anyway. You heard him. When you get Karl, ask him to tell Sheila I'm not up to skiing tonight."

"You're being very understanding, Nancy," Jody said, and she laughed. "Thank you."

Nancy said good night to Jody and let herself into her condo. Checking her watch, Nancy saw it was only eight-fifteen. She had almost two hours before Bess and George would show up.

"Maybe I will lie down," she said half out loud. Nancy lay on top of the goose-down comforter on her bed and immediately felt herself drift off to sleep.

* * *

Nancy woke up to the sound of the phone ringing and sunlight streaming in through her windows.

"Hello?" she mumbled, shaking her head to try to clear it. She couldn't believe how sick she still felt.

"Nancy?" Bess's voice cried. "Are you all right? We were told you got a bad case of food poisoning at the restaurant, and we decided not to disturb you last night."

Nancy explained that the doctor didn't think it was food poisoning. Bess's reaction was one of shock. "What was it, then?"

"I don't know," Nancy said. "I'll have to wait for the test results, I guess. Until I solve these cases, though, I'll have to be very careful."

"You think there's something else going on at Tall Pines besides the theft?" Bess asked.

"I'm sure of it." Nancy paused. "Someone locked us in that sauna. Someone switched the signs on the ski trail. I got dosed last night with something that made me very sick. Someone's after me, Bess. I'm sure of it."

"You think someone knows you're a detective and wants you out of here?" Bess asked in a low, breathless voice. "But who?"

"I don't know. Someone's found out. Or—"

"Or what?" Bess asked.

"Or someone simply wants to sabotage Tall Pines, and I've been the accidental victim each time," Nancy offered.

"Someone like Rob Watson, you mean," Bess said.

"Exactly."

After a short pause Bess asked, "What can George and I do to help?"

Nancy thought for a moment and then asked her friends to go to Jody's apartment, sneak in, and do a search of the girl's belongings. All three times that Nancy had been hurt Jody either had been there or had known where she was going to be. This made her highly suspicious. Could she have stolen the money and found out that Nancy was a detective? It was worth checking out.

"What are we looking for?" Bess asked.

"The rest of the fifty thousand dollars or some sign that Jody's made large deposits in her bank accounts recently," Nancy said. "Check to see if she really did go home yesterday between ten fifteen and ten forty-five," she added, remembering Jody's alibi.

"There's one problem," Bess told her. "I don't know how to break into an apartment."

Nancy had already thought of that. "Her mom should be at work, so try this: Tell the landlady you're planning a surprise party for Jody," she suggested. "Take some balloons. She'll probably let you in to decorate."

Bess giggled. "It just might work."

"Of course it will," Nancy promised.

Nancy lay down for a bit because she still felt awfully woozy, and she worked on a plan to check out Ben Wrobley. Slowly she got dressed and made her way to the building where the employees lived. She knew Ben taught at nine. It was five past now, so that gave her plenty of time to search his place. At the employees' complex Nancy found a directory out front.

Ben's apartment turned out to be at the far end of the building. The door was locked, but the lock was only a simple one, not a deadbolt. She pulled a credit card from her pocket and slid it along the doorjamb. A second later she was inside.

The apartment was just one room, she saw. Although small, it was well organized. A daybed with bolsters served as a couch, and cabinets over the desk provided additional storage. The back wall had a compact kitchenette and a door leading to a bath. Large skiing posters hung on the other three walls.

Nancy went to the desk first because it was the most logical place for Ben to hide whatever it was he'd taken from the office. She opened the top drawer. Nothing there but pens and pencils and a blank pad of paper. She leafed through the papers in the file drawer, but there were only copies of skiing articles from magazines.

She went over to search the storage bolsters above the bed, finding only blankets and pillows.

There was one hiding place left. Nancy walked across the room to the dresser. The first three drawers were filled with Ben's clothes. The last drawer held four hand-knit ski sweaters. Nancy slid her hand between each of the sweaters and then under the bottom one. Her fingers skidded on something smooth and flat.

A rush of excitement coursed through her as

she pulled the object out. She'd found a file folder—taken from Dave Kendall's office, no doubt.

Nancy checked the tab. "Inge Gustafson" was printed on it in neat black letters. Ben had stolen Inge's personnel file.

Sitting on the daybed, Nancy spread the folder open. As she started to read the letters and Inge's contract her eyes widened. No wonder Ben was so angry!

The Inge Gustafson Ski School was a sham. Karl had paid Inge a lump sum to use her name, but according to their agreement she had no further obligations—she didn't even have to give a single lesson!

Meanwhile Ben was doing all her work. He must have found out she was never going to show and taken this file as proof of his suspicions, Nancy figured. What was he going to do with the evidence, though?

As Nancy's thoughts spun through the possibilities she heard the rasp of a key in the lock. She searched frantically for a hiding spot, but before she could move, the door swung open. It was too late.

Nancy was caught!

Chapter

Nine

"WHAT ARE YOU DOING in my room?" Ben demanded, outraged.

Nancy knew that whatever she did, she couldn't blow her cover. "I saw you take something from Dave's office," she said. "I wanted to find out what it was."

Ben grabbed the folder from Nancy's hands. "You're not reviewing Tall Pines for a ski magazine, are you?" The look Ben gave Nancy was extremely skeptical.

Nancy decided that if her cover had to be blown, she might as well invent a better one—that of investigative reporter.

"Well, no, not exactly," she confessed, playing up her new role. "I'll tell you the truth—if you promise to keep it just between us."

Ben was obviously skeptical. "Okay."

"I heard about the theft a week ago, and I wanted to see if there was something going on at Tall Pines that the readers of *Tracks* should know about," she bluffed.

"So you're doing an exposé," Ben guessed.

"Exactly," Nancy told him. "But if anyone here finds out, I won't be able to learn a thing, and then"—she snapped her fingers—"end of story, right?"

Ben ran his hands through his jet black hair. "I see your point, but I still don't get why you searched my room. I didn't steal the money. Rebecca Montgomery did."

"I've interviewed her. She denies it, and I believe her," Nancy said, her hands on her hips.

Ben unzipped his parka and tossed it on the bed. "Then someone else took it."

Nancy gestured to the file lying beside Ben's jacket. "We both know that the Inge Gustafson Ski School is a sham. Maybe you wanted to get back at Karl for treating you so badly."

Ben's eyes blazed with anger. "Maybe I do want to get back at him, but I wouldn't steal from him. I'm not stupid." He paused. "You can get your story however you want," he went on angrily. "And when you do, you'll find out I'm innocent. Now I think you'd better go." With that Ben walked to the door and opened it. "Don't worry, though," he said quietly. "Your secret's safe with me."

Nancy smiled at the ski instructor. "Thank you," she said softly. She didn't know if Ben was telling her the truth—either about his not being the thief or about how he wouldn't tell anyone that she was "investigating" the theft at Tall Pines. Could she really believe him?

"Of course I understood," Sheila said when Nancy went to call on her at her condo. "Come in. Karl and I felt just awful when we heard what happened last night. Are you all right now?" she asked, her crystal blue eyes showing her concern.

Nancy's smile was brave, and Sheila wouldn't have guessed how queasy she still felt. "I'm fine, really," she fibbed gracefully. "I'd like to interview Karl if I could," she said after she and Sheila were seated on the couch. "Do you know when he'll be back?"

"I'm not sure," Sheila said. "He had some kind of problem to handle this morning." She tapped her fingers nervously on the arm of the couch. "My husband's too trusting. I mean, who else would hire a person with a criminal record?" she blurted out.

Sheila must have realized what she had let slip because her mouth instantly clamped shut. Before Nancy could question her further the phone rang, and at the same time there was a knock at the door.

"Would you get the phone?" Sheila asked Nancy as she hurried toward the door.

Nancy picked up the receiver that was on an end table beside the couch.

"I've got what you want," a man announced before Nancy could identify herself. "Meet me at that unfinished building tonight at ten." Without waiting for a response the man hung up. Nancy put the receiver down, completely puzzled by what she had just heard. Who was the man, and what did he have? What unfinished building was he talking about?

As she thought over the man's words Nancy remembered seeing Sheila the day before with the man in the black fedora by the new pond. There was an unfinished building there—the snack bar. Maybe the caller was the same man.

"Aren't these gorgeous?" Sheila came back into the room, her arms filled with flowers. "Karl sent them." She sniffed deeply.

"They're beautiful," Nancy agreed.

Sheila placed the floral arrangement in the middle of the coffee table and touched one of the petals. "This is a very rare iris," Sheila told Nancy as she sat down again. "Who was on the phone?" she asked, curious.

Nancy told her about the man's call, careful to watch the woman's reaction. "He didn't leave his name," she said.

Sheila flushed. She fingered the iris petal again, and Nancy could see her hand trembling. "He must have the anniversary gift I want for Karl." Sheila's words were spoken hesitantly, and her eyes never once met Nancy's.

Nancy had a strong suspicion Sheila was lying and decided to ask her about the day before. "Didn't I see you near the skating rink yesterday?" she asked. "I wanted to try it out but didn't know it wasn't finished yet."

The older woman's eyes narrowed. "No, it's

80

not done yet. You must have seen me there with the, uh, contractor. Karl asked me to meet him." With that she got up off the couch, picked up the flower arrangement, and nervously paced the room. "Now where should I put these?" she asked absently.

It was obvious to Nancy that the woman was hiding something. But what?

Sheila set the bouquet down on a nearby table and checked her watch. "Oh, Nancy, I'm so sorry," she said. "I just remembered I have an appointment in ten minutes, and I haven't even finished getting ready. Would you excuse me?" she asked, giving her a tense smile.

Nancy nodded and stood up. "Sure. Tell Karl I'll be in touch with him for that interview."

"Of course." As she held the door open for Nancy, Sheila smiled again. "Now, you take care of yourself," she said in a motherly tone.

Nancy smiled back and took off for her condo. She wanted to see if the doctor had left a message about what had caused her to pass out the night before.

When Nancy let herself into her condo the phone was ringing. She rushed to pick it up and heard Dr. Gorman identify himself on the other end. "I have the results of the tests," he said.

"And?" Nancy asked.

She heard Dr. Gorman clear his throat. "Nancy, I'm afraid your soup was poisoned."

"Poisoned!" Nancy closed her eyes and began to think. First the sauna, then the trail signs—those could have been pranks aimed at the resort,

81

not her. But poison? It was obvious now that someone was after her. Why, though?

"Nancy?" Dr. Gorman asked.

"Oh—I'm sorry," she said, then she paused. "Dr. Gorman, what kind of poison was it?"

"Convallatoxin," the doctor explained. "It's similar to digitalis, which is used to treat cardiac patients. That's why your heartbeat was so slow. What I can't tell you is how it was administered."

"Is it a powder?" Nancy asked, trying to imagine how someone had gotten the poison into her soup.

"No. The original source is a plant, but the lab didn't find any evidence of flower parts. They think the poison was a liquid."

Nancy thought for a moment. "There were flowers on the table," she said. "Someone accidentally nudged the table, and the vase tipped over."

"Some of the water might have splashed into your bowl," Dr. Gorman concluded. "What kind of flowers were they?"

"Lilies of the valley."

Nancy heard him turning the pages of a book.

"That's it!" the doctor cried. "Lilies of the valley are highly poisonous. Even the water they've been standing in can cause serious illness."

"Are you sure?" Nancy asked.

"Yes," he said. "But that's good news. The poisoning must have been accidental."

It was a comforting theory, but Nancy had a strong feeling that it was wrong. The poisoning had been no accident. The vase of flowers had been in the center of the table, too far from her bowl for an accidental spill to reach her soup.

Nancy thanked the doctor and hung up, her mind reeling. There was no doubt about it. Someone had deliberately poisoned her, someone who knew about flowers.

Still, after all her investigating, Nancy had been unable to narrow her list of suspects. Now Dr. Gorman's diagnosis had made the case even more complex.

Nancy had a new suspect: Sheila Reismueller.

Chapter

Ten

THE CASE NOW HAD a new angle. Not many people at Tall Pines knew enough about flowers to know that lilies of the valley could be poisonous. But Sheila Reismueller would have that kind of knowledge. She had also picked up the flowers and rearranged them when they were knocked over.

But why would Sheila want to poison her?

If the resort owner's wife knew Nancy was a detective investigating the theft, and if Sheila was hiding something about the theft, that would give her a reason to poison Nancy.

But that was a lot of ifs. Maybe there wasn't any connection at all between the theft and the poisoning.

Sheila's nervousness around Nancy *was* suspicious, though. Nancy didn't believe Sheila's explanation about the phone call, either. But what was she hiding? It made no sense.

With a sigh Nancy picked up the phone. One thing she could do was check on the Tall Pines employees. She wanted to find out who at the resort had a record. Sheila had said someone did. There was a chance that that person had slipped and committed another crime.

Within a few minutes Nancy was connected to Chief McGinnis of the River Heights Police Department. With a little convincing Nancy was able to get him to run a trace on her main suspects: Ben Wrobley, Jody Ashton, and—just to be on the safe side—Sheila Reismueller. The chief agreed to contact her as soon as he found out anything.

Almost as soon as Nancy hung up the phone she heard a knock on the door. Bess and George were back.

"You were right!" Bess exclaimed, grinning. Obviously they were pleased with their investigation. "When we told Jody's landlady we were planning a surprise party for her, she let us into the apartment." Bess chuckled. "Those balloons were worth their weight in gold."

"So what did you learn?"

Bess's smile faded as she and George entered the condo. "Not much. We couldn't find the money anywhere. We searched everything."

"How about bankbooks? Did you find them?"

"There was only one savings book," George said, "and that didn't have any big deposits.

Jody's been putting in small, regular amounts every payday."

"That seems to back up Jody's story that she's saving money for college," Nancy said, thinking out loud.

"The only strange transaction was one Jody made—a big withdrawal," Bess said, tossing back her long blond hair.

That *was* strange. "How much?" Nancy asked.

"Two thousand dollars," George answered. She sank into the sofa and let out a long sigh. "It doesn't seem like we're getting anywhere on this case," she said, shaking her head. "Rebecca's been calling me to find out how we're doing. What can I tell her, Nan?"

"You can't tell her much, but I guess you can say my cover's blown, and that someone tried to poison me last night," Nancy said.

"Nancy!" Bess cried. "Are you joking?"

George's eyes became round. "Poison?"

Nancy nodded and quickly told her friends about the lab results. "So the culprit has to know something about flowers. Any sign that Jody does?"

George looked at Bess, and they both shook their heads. "Ben doesn't, either," George said.

"That leaves Sheila. . . ." A thought nagged at Nancy. Who else at Tall Pines knew about flowers? Then it hit her. "And Dave Kendall!"

It was ten-fifty, and Nancy had almost forgotten her eleven o'clock appointment with Dave. She grabbed her jacket and headed for the door.

"See you at the snack bar for lunch?" she asked. "Twelve?"

"Sure," George said, confused. "Anything else we can do?"

"Nope!" With that Nancy waved goodbye and was on her way to Dave Kendall's office. Since she'd arranged to interview him anyway, she thought, this would be a great opportunity to find out exactly how much he knew about flowers.

When Nancy entered Dave's office the general manager was standing in front of a filing cabinet.

"Hi," Nancy said as she entered the office. "Ready for our interview?"

Dave turned around, and Nancy saw that he was holding a small trowel. Light streamed through the windows onto the masses of orchids. "Just give me a second to finish potting this, and I'll be with you."

Dave brushed off his hands and sat down behind his desk. "Now what can I do for you?" he asked. "I hope you're enjoying your stay here."

"I am." Nancy glanced at the orchids. "Those flowers are beautiful," she said. "Do you grow anything else?"

Dave leaned back in his chair and smiled. "I've tried, but my green thumb seems limited to orchids. Strange, because most people find that they're the hardest to grow."

"It is strange," Nancy agreed, turning back to him. She cleared her throat and took out her notepad. "It seems that your prankster has struck

87

again," she said. Then she went on to explain the details of her poisoning the night before. "I know my editor is going to want some reassurance that things are under control at Tall Pines before we print any review. Do you have a comment?"

Dave was silent for a moment, giving Nancy the impression he was carefully weighing his words. "From what you say, it sounds like an accident—an unfortunate one, to be sure, but still an accident. The vase overturned, and obviously water splashed into your soup." He paused. "You have my personal assurance that everything here at Tall Pines is in order. Any other questions?"

Nancy tapped her pencil on her notebook. Dave's explanation didn't take into account what had happened in the sauna or on the ski trail. His manner was professional, but he could easily be hiding something.

She spent a few more minutes posing questions that she thought a reporter for *Tracks* might ask. Dave easily answered her questions about their expansion plans and advertising campaign, showing little nervousness or concern that she might be anything more than a reporter. If he suspected she was a detective, he didn't show it.

Nancy realized she wasn't going to get much more out of Dave Kendall and finished up the interview. "Thanks for your time," she said, standing to leave.

"No problem," Dave said. He gave her a polite smile and a firm handshake. "You must be almost done with your story."

Nancy packed her notebook and pencil and headed for the door. "Almost," she told him.

"That's good," he said, holding the door for her. "And don't worry about these accidents. In my experience, when a resort first opens there are always a few wrinkles to iron out."

Nancy thanked him and left, thinking that what was happening at Tall Pines was a lot more serious than a "few wrinkles." She made her way to the snack bar to meet Bess and George and wondered along the way why Dave Kendall was so reluctant to take the accidents seriously. Was it simply his wanting to reassure her because she was a reporter, or was the man trying to cover something up?

Just as Nancy was coming up to the ski shop she saw an expensive-looking green sports car pull into the main parking lot. From the spotless shine and the temporary plates Nancy could tell that it was brand-new.

She admired the sleek lines of the car as the driver steered it into an empty space, stopped, and got out.

Nancy's mouth fell open in amazement. The person getting out of the brand-new sports car was none other than Jody Ashton!

Chapter

Eleven

JODY PATTED THE FENDER of the car before carefully locking the door. As she turned she saw Nancy.

"Isn't it the best?" she asked, tossing her keys in the air. "I just picked it up. I can't believe it's mine—finally. Wow!" she said under her breath, gazing at the car one last time.

"It's gorgeous," Nancy agreed. She ran her eyes over the car and calculated to herself what it must have cost. Even if Jody had had enough for a down payment from her savings account, how could she possibly afford the monthly payments if she was saving for college? Unless she'd just come into some money—like fifty thousand dollars from the Tall Pines payroll, for example.

"There's a sleigh ride at dusk today," Jody was saying. "Are you going?"

Nancy's thoughts were still on Jody's brand-new car. She nodded absently. "I wouldn't miss it."

"Well, I'd better get back to the shop," Jody said. "See you later!" She waved and walked off toward the main building.

Nancy made her way to the snack bar, mulling over this latest development. What if Jody had taken the money and found out Nancy was investigating the theft? The girl would have a good reason for trying to get her off the case. Jody had known she was going to the sauna and that Nancy and Bess were going to ski Aerie. Only her theory didn't account for the fact that, as far as she knew, Jody didn't know enough about flowers to poison her. Sheila was still her number-one suspect for the poisoning.

Nancy glanced around the snack shop for Bess and George. The room was filled with guests, but there was no sign of Nancy's friends. She decided to check out the gift shop and ski school.

As she opened the door to the ski school Nancy immediately saw George standing in front of the counter talking to Ben. There was no sign of Bess.

After Ben and George finished their conversation Ben went over to his locker. Nancy shot George a warning look and asked casually, "How are the trails this morning?"

"Great," Ben said. "The fresh snow last night really helped— That's odd," he said, interrupting himself.

"Is something wrong, Ben?" George asked.

Ben was standing next to his locker, a puzzled

91

expression on his face, holding a bunch of white flowers. Nancy raced over to Ben. "Can I see those?" she asked, reaching for the flowers.

It was a bouquet of wilted lilies of the valley!

Ben just stared at Nancy, his confusion obvious. Finally he handed her the flowers.

"Do you know what these are?" Nancy asked.

Ben shrugged his shoulders. "They look like dead white flowers." He sounded genuinely puzzled.

"They're lilies of the valley," Nancy said, watching Ben's face.

"So?" Once again Ben's voice was casual. He seemed to have no idea of the flowers' significance.

"What's wrong?" George asked innocently. Nancy could see in her friend's eyes that George was as surprised as she was to see the flowers.

"Last night someone tried to poison me with lilies of the valley," Nancy explained.

George gasped. "You're kidding," she said, pretending to be surprised to protect Nancy's cover. "You're the reporter, aren't you?" When Nancy nodded, George asked, "Why would someone try to poison you?"

Ben grew pale. "Don't look at me!" he cried.

"These *were* in your locker," Nancy said, holding out the flowers. "They didn't get in there by magic."

Ben pointed at his locker. "Check it out," he said. "It wouldn't take Houdini to pick this lock. Anyone could have put those flowers in there."

"But why?" George asked, wrinkling her nose.

"This is totally strange. How would anyone know other people would be around when you opened your locker? It makes no sense that anyone, including you, would stash those flowers in your locker. Why not just throw them out?"

"Maybe someone wanted to frame me," Ben suggested. "Or at least make it look like I could be guilty."

Nancy was quickly assessing the situation. Ben's actions weren't those of a guilty person. He'd seemed honestly confused by the flowers. She was beginning to think the ski instructor was telling her the truth about them. Also, Ben was right—anyone could have broken into his locker and planted the lilies. But why? Why would anyone do something like that?

Ben grabbed his jacket from the locker and slipped into it. "I've got a lesson," he explained. "Sorry I can't stick around. See you later this afternoon, George?" he asked with a raised eyebrow. "Say, three o'clock?"

"Perfect," George said, beaming at him as he left.

"Ski lesson?" Nancy asked. George's smile indicated that there might be something more than skiing going on between the two of them.

George started to blush. "Something like that. Come on," she said. "I'm starving!"

At around seven that night Nancy and Bess joined the crowd that had gathered in front of the lodge for the sleigh ride.

"Look at all these furs," Bess said, wrinkling

her nose at the coats many people had on. "Think of all those poor animals—" She shuddered and didn't finish the thought.

George came up to Nancy and Bess just then. "Good day on the trails?" Nancy asked with a wink.

"Perfect!" George said as the sound of bells filled the air. The crowd became silent and turned to watch the sleighs approach.

"This is going to be fun," Bess said excitedly, clapping her hands together as the sleighs drew closer. There were seven of them, all painted black. Two horses harnessed to each sleigh pulled them up to the crowd of guests. Tall Pines drivers held the horses in check with forest green harnesses.

"Let's ride with Ben," George suggested when she saw him driving the lead sleigh, but the girls were too late. Other guests piled into the first six sleighs, leaving Nancy, Bess, and George to climb into the last one.

The girls wrapped their legs in woolen blankets, and each draped another one around her shoulders. Their driver, a thin blond woman with her hair pulled back in a ponytail, smiled at them. "Ready?" she asked.

Bess beamed at her. "You bet!"

"Heeyah!" the woman said, snapping the reins. With that they skimmed along on the snow and entered the woods. The sleighs in front of them were barely visible through the thick pines, and the only sounds were the steady beats of horses' hooves, the jingle of sleigh bells, and the lulling whoosh of sleigh runners over the hard-packed snow.

A clump of snow fell into their sleigh from one of the overhanging pine boughs. Bess shivered and pulled her blanket tighter around her. "This is a little spooky, huh?"

"I think it's beautiful," George said, lifting her eyes to the darkening night sky.

They rode without speaking for a few minutes, then George broke the silence and pointed to an area just ahead of them. "That's a great trail for night skiing." She turned to Nancy. "Let's try it tomorrow."

"You two go right ahead." Bess snuggled deeper into her blankets. "This is my idea of a terrific winter sport."

The sleigh took a path that ran beside a trail. Nancy saw two men on the trail skiing in parallel tracks, moving quickly and gracefully.

"Good, aren't they?" Nancy asked, pointing the skiers out to George.

Her friend followed Nancy's gaze and nodded. "Almost professional," she said.

As the sleigh drew closer Nancy studied the skiers' backs. Moonlight filtered in through the trees and shone brightly on the shorter of the two men. Nancy knew she'd seen him before. There was no mistaking that head of white hair. It was Rob Watson.

What was Watson doing skiing on Tall Pines's trails? Checking out the competition, or had he come back to cause more trouble?

Nancy felt adrenaline rush through her. The

man Rob was with had on a Tall Pines jacket. Who could he be?

She strained her eyes, trying to get a better look at Rob's companion.

Finally the taller man turned his face toward their sleigh, and Nancy gasped at who it was.

It was Dave Kendall!

Chapter

Twelve

NANCY WHISPERED, pointing at the two skiers, "It's Rob Watson and Dave Kendall."

"Rob Watson and Dave Kendall!" George practically shouted. "What are those two doing hanging out together?"

Nancy's thoughts quickly went back to when she'd caught Watson entering the Tall Pines offices. What if Rob had had an appointment to see Dave and hadn't been breaking in? He might have taken off because Nancy saw him and not because he was afraid Dave would catch him. Dave's acting angry at Rob could have just been a bluff to throw Nancy off his track.

"Maybe Dave's giving him a tour of the trails," Bess suggested.

George's eyes narrowed. "At night? Somehow I don't think so," she said. "Nancy, are you thinking what I'm thinking?" she asked.

Nancy nodded. "There aren't many reasons for the general manager of Tall Pines to be meeting a competitor unless they're working together," she said. Nancy quickly explained how she'd seen Watson in Dave's office.

"Watson's renovations!" George said. "What if Dave stole the money and split it with Rob?"

"But why?" Bess asked.

George leaned forward to get the attention of the woman driving the sleigh. "Would you mind stopping?" she asked. "I'd like to take a walk in the woods."

"A walk?" Nancy and Bess asked as their driver reined in the horses and the sleigh came to a halt.

George hopped out of the sleigh. "I'm going to follow Rob and Dave."

"That's crazy," Nancy said. "We can't possibly catch up to them on foot. Or do you have a plan?"

George's grin told her all she had to know. "Coming, Bess?"

Bess shook her head and tucked the blanket in tight around her. "You guys go ahead. I'll meet you back at the condo, okay?"

Nancy and George waved a quick goodbye as the sleigh started to move again. "This way." George motioned to Nancy to follow her as she started to run alongside the ski tracks. Rob and Dave were skiing at a good pace and were almost out of sight.

"I still don't think we have a chance," Nancy said, falling to her knees in a deep snowdrift.

"They're on skis. How can we possibly catch them?"

She searched down the trail and could just make out Rob and Dave as they made their way around a far bend.

"There's a way, Nan. I promise you. I've skied this trail before. It bends to the right and goes deeper into the woods. Then it bends back," she told Nancy. "If we cut straight through this meadow here, we should be able to cut them off."

"George, you're a genius!" Nancy said. "Let's go!"

They left the trail and rushed across the meadow. The snow had a thick crust that kept them from sinking in. Soon they'd crossed the meadow and were back in the woods. George pulled Nancy behind a tree next to the trail, and both girls held their breath, waiting for Dave and Rob to reappear.

George studied the tracks. "They haven't come yet," she said, pointing to the light dusting of snow in the tracks. "The snow would be packed if someone had skied on it."

Nancy kept her eyes on the trail, but Dave and Rob were nowhere in sight. The minutes ticked by, and still they didn't show. "They should be here by now," George said, checking her watch.

"Let's wait a little longer," Nancy said. But fifteen minutes passed, and Dave and Rob still hadn't skied past them. Nancy tried to control her disappointment. "They must have turned off the trail," she said. She stomped her foot in frustration. "Another dead end!"

"Maybe they went back to Dave's office," George suggested. "Let's head over there and see."

"George, you're full of great ideas tonight!" Nancy hugged her friend and stepped out of the woods onto the trail. "Even if Dave isn't there, we can check out his office. The last time I searched, the receptionist interrupted me before I could finish."

When they reached the administration building they saw that all the lights were off. "Looks like they didn't come back here," George said, biting her lower lip.

"That's okay," Nancy said. Her frustration had melted away. Being able to search Dave's office was something, at least. She reached into the belt pack she wore around her waist. She pulled out her lock-pick kit and a pocket flashlight. Within a minute she'd opened the front door. The door to Dave's office was easy enough to unlock, and within another minute she had that open, too.

Nancy switched on the flashlight and closed the door behind them.

"What first?" George asked.

"The personnel files," Nancy said. "Sheila told me Karl had hired someone with a record. Chief McGinnis is searching, but he hasn't called yet. Maybe we'll find the evidence we need here in one of the files."

Nancy moved to the first of the cabinets and opened the drawer. George went to the other and started checking. Thumbing through the hanging folders, Nancy quickly found the section with the personnel files.

"Ashton, Jody," Nancy read on the first file. Inside she found letters of recommendation and Jody's employment application. Nancy flipped through it and discovered that the last page of the application was missing. Strange. Nancy checked another employee file. Sure enough, Jody's application was missing a list of previous employers and a signed statement that she had never been convicted of a criminal offense.

"Find something?" George asked.

"I'm not sure." Nancy handed George Jody's file and pointed out what was missing. While George flipped through it, Nancy reached for Dave's folder. She leafed through the recommendations and pulled out his application, which was complete, unlike Jody's. Nancy turned to the back page and glanced at his previous job experience. Nothing unusual, except there was a two-year gap right before he'd joined Tall Pines.

George was back at the other cabinet. "One of these files is empty," George said.

"What kind?" Nancy asked.

"It's a bank file," George told her. "Monroe Savings and Loan."

"Maybe it's misfiled. The folder could be with the other bank records," Nancy suggested. "Keep looking."

Nancy went back to checking the employee files but didn't turn up anything new. George was still flipping through the other file cabinet.

"Something is definitely wrong here, Nancy,"

George said. "This bank folder is the only one, and it's empty. There aren't any other bank records here at all, even though this is where all the rest of the accounting stuff is."

Nancy peered over George's shoulder. "Karl's office?" she wondered.

"Let's check it out," George agreed.

Within a minute Nancy and George were inside Karl Reismueller's office. Nancy ran the flashlight over the dim interior.

"This looks more like someone's living room than an office," George said in an astonished tone.

With its plush carpet, long leather couch, and mahogany desk and credenza the office was quite elegant. Nancy went toward Karl's desk while George made for the credenza.

"Nothing here," George announced a few minutes later. She sounded discouraged.

"Nothing in the desk, either." Nancy was thoughtful. "How can you run a ski resort without any bank records?" she wondered aloud.

"It's not that there aren't any," George said. "The empty folder proves that. It's just that we can't find them."

Nancy scanned the room one last time, her gaze landing on a mahogany wall unit that matched Karl's sleek, modern desk. She went to it and pulled open the doors, revealing a personal computer.

"Maybe this is our answer." Nancy switched on the computer and pulled a chair over. The machine made a soft whirring noise for a few seconds, then it flashed a message.

"'Please enter password,'" George read over Nancy's shoulder. "If this is like most systems, we've got only three chances. After that it'll lock up."

Nancy thought for a moment. "Most people pick a password they won't have trouble remembering. What about 'Pines'?"

She typed in the word and pressed the Enter key. "Invalid password. Please try again," the system responded.

They had two more chances.

"How about 'Karl'?" George suggested. "It is his name—chances are, he wouldn't forget it."

Nancy laughed and typed in the name. "'Invalid password. Please try again,'" came the reply.

Neither George nor Nancy spoke, but they both knew they had only one more chance. Nancy closed her eyes and tried to think. "What's the most important thing in Karl Reismueller's life?"

George thought for a moment. "His wife!"

Nancy smiled and typed in "Sheila." The computer began to whir.

"We did it!" George crowed as a menu appeared on the monitor.

"Let's try the general ledger system," Nancy said, entering the code from the menu. Another menu appeared, asking her which company records she wanted to see.

"Wow! Karl owns a lot of companies." George started to read the list of names. "All-State Printing, Toys-for-All, Well-Heeled Cobbler. Is there any business he's not in?"

Nancy selected Tall Pines and began reviewing the financial information. "There are a lot of loans," she told George as they studied the screen. "Actually, I'm not surprised. That's pretty normal for the first year in business."

"What about the other companies?"

Nancy returned to the menu and asked for information about Karl's printing company. She stared at the screen for a minute, then inquired about the chain of toy stores. The answer was the same for each.

"Every one of these companies has borrowed money to the limit," she said. "I don't understand. If he's doing well, he shouldn't have so many loans. Where's Karl's Midas touch that everyone talks about?"

"Do you think he's in financial trouble?" George asked.

"It sure seems like it." Nancy flipped to another screen. "More debt. Opening Tall Pines must have strained Karl's finances to the breaking point. Hey"—Nancy looked up at George—"I just remembered. The other night at dinner Sheila was about to say something about money problems when Karl cut her off."

George nodded her understanding. "No wonder Karl was so upset by the theft. He couldn't afford to lose fifty thousand dollars."

"That was covered by insurance," Nancy reminded her. "But the rest of Karl's businesses don't seem to be doing well, either."

"I wish we could find the bank records," George said. "They might explain a lot."

"We still don't know why they're missing," Nancy agreed. "Or who took them." She scrolled through several screens but couldn't find a single menu directing her to Tall Pines' bank records.

George leaned over her shoulder and watched while Nancy worked. "So what does this all mean?" she asked.

"Reismueller has financial problems," Nancy said, leaning back in her chair. "Someone's got the bank records. That someone could be Dave."

"I don't follow," George said. "You're way ahead of me."

"What if Dave is working with Watson, and they stole the money to cause Karl trouble?" Nancy suggested. She was piecing together her theory as she spoke.

"But you just said he got the money back from the insurance company, so I think that whoever stole the money really needed it. I don't think that person was just causing Karl trouble," George said.

"That's true," Nancy agreed. "But Dave and Watson could still be working together. The money for renovations, and the sabotage to drive people away from Tall Pines."

"But how's that connected to the records?" George asked.

Nancy thought for a moment. "Dave could be holding the records as a way of blackmailing

Karl. Maybe Karl found out about the theft and threatened to turn Dave in."

"I guess that makes sense," George said. She bit on a fingernail. "Still, it doesn't really explain why someone tried to poison you specifically and why all the attacks have been made against you."

George had a point. So far Nancy didn't have any proof that Dave was capable of poisoning her. The only person who had the knowledge to do that was—

"Sheila!" Nancy cried. "I completely forgot." She rushed to turn off the computer and pick up her flashlight. "Come on, George."

"You completely forgot what?" George asked, following Nancy out of Karl's office.

Nancy told George about Sheila's appointment with the strange man who'd called earlier that day at the Reismuellers' condo. "It's almost ten now. We've got to get to the skating pond."

"What does it mean?" George asked.

Outside the administrative offices a light snow had begun to fall, and it was pitch-black. "I don't know," Nancy answered, "but I'm going to be there to find out." She started walking in the direction of the pond.

"I'm coming with you," George announced.

"I don't think that's such a good idea," Nancy said. "Bess is probably worried about us."

George ran her hands through her dark curls. "I don't know, Nancy. You might be in danger."

"It won't be the first time," Nancy said with a laugh.

"Okay." George took a deep breath. "Just promise me you'll be careful."

"Aren't I always?" Nancy said. With that she said goodbye to George, arranging to meet back at George and Bess's room at the main lodge.

In a few minutes Nancy had reached the skating pond. The whole area between the pond and the snack bar was dark, lit only by the moon and stars. As Nancy approached the unfinished snack bar she checked carefully in all directions. No sign of either Sheila or the man. She sprinted the last few yards and stood outside the door of the building, listening carefully. There was no sound, and the building seemed empty. Carefully she eased open the door and slipped inside.

Nancy looked around, searching for a place to hide. Her eyes lit on a pile of wood paneling stacked along one wall. Perfect! If she hid behind it, she'd be able to hear the conversation without being seen.

She moved toward the paneling. As she did she heard a sound coming from behind her. Someone else was in the snack bar!

Nancy turned, but it was too late. She saw a tall, dark figure, a raised arm. Before she could move there was an instant of blinding pain, then darkness.

Chapter
Thirteen

NANCY MOANED SOFTLY as she came to in the cold and dark, not sure where she was. Then memory rushed back. She had come to the snack bar to find Sheila and the stranger. Instead, someone had found her.

Sitting up, Nancy held her head in her hands, trying to fight the wave of dizziness and nausea that came from the throbbing pain at the back of her head. That must have been where she was hit. The dizziness passed, and Nancy took in her surroundings. The building appeared to be empty. There was no sign of Sheila or the man, nothing to indicate that anyone else had been there except the faint scent of perfume.

Nancy took a deep whiff and frowned. The fragrance was unmistakable. As far as she knew, only one person at Tall Pines wore that spicy mixture of roses and lilies: Sheila Reismueller.

It had happened so quickly that Nancy hadn't recognized the person who hit her. She didn't even know if her assailant had been a man or a woman. It could have been Sheila, the man she was meeting, or anyone else, though Nancy doubted the third possibility. All she knew for sure was that someone didn't want her nosing around at Tall Pines.

As Nancy stood up her foot kicked a hard object, and she bent down to pick it up. It was a flashlight. She was pretty sure it hadn't been there when she'd come into the snack bar. It must be what she had been struck with, Nancy thought, slipping the flashlight into her belt pack.

She made her way out of the building, on the watch for Sheila or the man she'd been meeting. Nancy figured they were both long gone—she wasn't sure how much time had passed—but she needed to be sure. The question was, which of them had knocked her out, and why?

"How'd it go?" George asked when Nancy appeared at their door.

Nancy took off her coat and sat cross-legged on one of the beds. "To make a bad pun," she said with a smile, "it was a stunning experience."

After Nancy explained what had happened, Bess was truly alarmed. "Nancy, I'm worried. There's a criminal running around, and he's determined to hurt you. First the poison, now this."

"I think 'he' is a 'she,' " Nancy told her friends. "Sheila knows enough about flowers to have poured the water in my soup, and that was definitely her perfume I smelled. But I still don't understand what Sheila doesn't want me to know. It didn't make sense that she would be involved in stealing from her husband's resort. The success of Tall Pines seemed so important to Sheila."

"Maybe the meeting between her and the stranger had to do with Karl's shaky finances," George suggested. At Bess's perplexed expression George told her cousin what she and Nancy had found out in their search through Karl's computer earlier.

"Wow!" Bess said. Then her expression changed. "I don't get it, though. What could Sheila possibly have to do with the missing bank records or the theft?"

Nancy explained her theory about Dave's blackmailing Karl with the bank records. "Maybe Sheila was meeting with someone who was going to take care of the Reismuellers' problem with Dave," she suggested.

"You don't mean . . ." George asked, her voice trailing off.

"Getting rid of him and Rob . . ." Nancy shook her head to clear her thoughts. "The only way to find out is to confront Sheila or trick her into revealing what's going on." She pulled the flashlight out of her belt pack. "I found this on the ground next to me. I think she or the man she was meeting used it to knock me out."

"You're not going to show it to her, are you?" George asked, deadly serious. "If you're right about your suspicions, it could be dangerous to confront her."

"George is right, Nancy." Bess got up from the couch and paced the room. "Sheila could be trouble. Besides, if you're going to confront anyone, it should be Dave Kendall. If your theory is right, Dave's the one behind all the attacks."

Nancy thought for a moment. Bess and George had a point—if Dave really was the thief. She still hadn't ruled Jody out as a suspect, though. That brand-new car didn't fit with her saving for college. Thinking about it, she realized she didn't have enough clues to confront anyone.

She let out a long sigh. "I guess you're right," she admitted. "Besides, it's too late to do anything."

"What can we help with tomorrow?" George asked eagerly.

"I want you to check out Jody," Nancy said. She told her friends about Jody's new car. "Call around and try to find out whether or not she paid cash. I'll check out Dave."

Bess put her arm around Nancy. "Don't worry," she said as if she sensed Nancy's frustration. "We still have a couple of days to get to the bottom of this."

When Nancy woke up the next morning she saw that the message light on her phone was lit. She dialed the operator, who told her that George and Bess had had to make an emergency trip home. Apparently something had happened to

Bess's parents, and the cousins had left first thing that morning.

Nancy showered and got dressed. She tried calling the Marvins' house, but there was no answer. As she left her condo she found herself hoping that everything was okay with Bess and George. She realized, though, that there was nothing she could do to help them. She had her hands full trying to help herself.

Nancy decided to start with Jody since Bess and George couldn't. She was heading past the ski shop on her way to the main building when she heard a familiar voice.

"Just the person I wanted to see," Ben called. "Come on into the ski school."

Nancy followed him inside and over to the ski school counter. He pulled a pair of skis and poles from behind the counter. "Look what I've got for you." He handed Nancy the set, along with boots and a folded sheet of paper.

"It's from Jody," Nancy said as she read the typewritten note dated the day before. "She said the equipment's from the latest shipment." Looking at Ben, Nancy asked, "Do you know where Jody is? I want to thank her." She also wanted to question Jody, but she didn't want to tell Ben that.

"It's her day off," Ben answered. "Sometimes she comes here and skis, but I think I heard her say something about staying home today."

Nancy tried to hide her disappointment. She'd have to find Dave first now. She thanked Ben and asked if he could keep her new equipment there for her. "I have a few things to do. Maybe I'll be back later to ski."

"No problem," Ben said, putting the equipment against the wall behind the counter. "Let me know if you want another lesson."

Nancy excused herself and went to the administration building to find Dave. But when she reached the office, both his door and Karl's were closed and locked.

"I think Dave's out skiing this morning," the receptionist said in response to Nancy's question. "If you want to see him, you might try the Cascades trail. It's one of his favorites."

Nancy hustled back to the ski school to pick up her equipment. Outside she tightened her boots into the ski bindings and slid her hands into the pole straps, then skied gracefully to the trail head.

For a few minutes Nancy just concentrated on skiing. The new skis were shorter and the poles longer than the ones she had used before. Ben had told her it would be the perfect equipment for skating, but it took Nancy a few minutes to feel comfortable with it. Soon, though, she was gliding along the trail, pushing off with her left ski and gliding on the right as Ben had taught her. There was no doubt about it. The new equipment was terrific, and she was soon skiing at a fast clip.

The beginning of the trail was easy, and her arms and legs were moving in a tight, comfortable rhythm. Nancy kept her eyes peeled for

Dave, and as soon as Aerie split off she took Cascades. After only a few minutes on the trail Nancy spotted a man with a Tall Pines jacket in the distance. She put on the speed, sure that it must be Dave Kendall. When there was only twenty feet between them Nancy called out his name.

"Dave! Wait for me!"

The man turned—it was Dave. Instead of slowing his stride, though, Dave quickened it, shooting farther away from her.

Nancy wasn't going to let him get away that easily. She slid both skis into the tracks and resumed a diagonal stride. She stretched her right arm out, gaining the maximum distance she could with her pole. As she pushed off with all her might, pulling the pole behind her, her other arm swung forward.

The distance between Nancy and Dave shortened. She reached forward again, putting more power into her poling. It was the only way she knew to gain real speed. If she could just keep going, she'd catch him.

With a final burst of energy Nancy began to double-pole. She reached forward with both poles at the same time, pushing off with every ounce of energy she could muster. The trail dived down into a deep forest. Dave was closer. In a few more strokes she'd be down the slope next to him. She reached forward and dug her poles into the snow.

Then suddenly, without warning, Nancy felt herself fall forward. One minute she was skiing—the next, the binding on her right ski had snapped open.

Nancy tried to control herself, but it was no use. She fell to the ground, head over heels—and started rolling and tumbling downhill, headed straight for a huge tree.

Chapter

Fourteen

NANCY CONTINUED to hurtle through the air. Moving instinctively, she tucked her body into a ball and shifted her weight to the right.

It worked! Nancy rolled in the snow and slid to a stop just inches from the tree.

"Are you okay?" Dave Kendall's skis sprayed snow as he stopped next to Nancy.

She took a moment to catch her breath, then stood up carefully. "I'm fine," she answered, brushing the snow off.

Before she could say anything more Dave headed back up the trail. When he returned a minute later he was carrying Nancy's skis under one arm. "These must be yours," he said as he handed them to her.

Nancy took the skis and checked them out. There didn't seem to be anything wrong with the binding that had snapped open, no reason why it should have failed. But as Nancy looked more closely she saw that the front screw, the one that held the binding to the ski, was missing. It must have been loose when she started up the trail, and the extra force she put on the skis racing downhill toward Dave had caused it to come out.

"You could have been seriously hurt," Dave said when Nancy showed him the binding.

Nancy gave Dave a long look before she spoke. "I've been involved in an awful lot of 'accidents' since I came to Tall Pines," she said. "A jammed sauna door, mysteriously switched trail signs, poisoned soup, and now a broken binding. I'm beginning to wonder why someone's trying to hurt me."

"I guess you never thought being a reporter could be such a dangerous profession," Dave said, raising his eyebrow. "Or that a ski resort could be such a treacherous place."

With that, Dave turned around in the trail and started to ski off, leaving Nancy to walk back by herself. Nancy instantly weighed the consequences of dropping her cover. It was something she had to do if she was going to get anywhere with him and her questioning.

"I'm not a reporter, Dave," she called to him evenly.

He turned around to face her, his nervousness and anxiety apparent. "You're not?" he asked.

Nancy let her ski drop to the ground. "No. I'm a detective."

"A detective!" Dave let loose a peal of laughter. "A detective!"

This was hardly the response Nancy had expected. "What's so funny?" she asked, studying him curiously.

"This whole time I thought you were a reporter." He paused. "Aren't you awfully young to be a detective?" he asked.

"Not really," Nancy told him, crossing her arms. "You still haven't explained what's so funny."

Suddenly Dave got serious. "Nothing."

Nancy paused. "It wouldn't have anything to do with that missing bank file, would it?" she asked.

Before Dave could answer, two skiers came down the trail, and Dave stepped out of their way. As soon as they had passed, Nancy asked him again about the file that was missing from his office. "Where is it, Dave?" she asked. "What's in it that made you take the file? Does Rob Watson have it?" she bluffed.

At Watson's name Dave shot Nancy an angry look. "What do you know about Watson?"

"Only that I saw you skiing with him last night," Nancy told him. "And that I suspect the two of you are behind my 'accidents.'"

"What makes you say that?" Dave asked. He leaned on his ski poles and narrowed his eyes. "What if I told you I was just giving Rob a friendly tour of our state-of-the-art trails?"

"That doesn't explain what he was doing in the administration building the other night," Nancy said, meeting his glance. "Or why you've always been near whenever I've almost been injured."

Nancy ticked off the evidence on her fingers. "Fact: You knew I was going to take a sauna. Fact: You came by my table the night I was poisoned. I'd say it's probably even a fact that you and Rob stole the money from Tall Pines and framed Rebecca for it—"

"That's enough!" Dave stopped her. He held up a gloved hand and shook his head slowly. "I'll tell you the truth. I did block that sauna door, and I even switched the trail signs. I came by the ski shop right after you and that girl went up on the trails. Ben told me you were skiing Aerie. I came up Cascades and switched the signs."

"But why?" Nancy asked. "Lots of people could have gotten hurt, not just Bess."

Dave hung his head for a moment, then finally looked at Nancy. "I believed that you were a reporter," he said, giving Nancy a weak smile, "not a detective. I wanted you to give Tall Pines a rotten write-up. The best way to guarantee that was to cause trouble for you. But I never meant for anything serious to happen—you have to believe me."

"The poisoning wasn't serious?" Nancy emphasized the last word. "You could have killed me!"

"I dribbled only a couple of drops of the water in your soup when I stood the vase up," Dave explained. "It was enough to make you sick but not seriously harm you. And I knew someone would come along when you were locked in the sauna. As far as the trails are concerned, I didn't know your friend was a novice skier."

"What about these?" Nancy asked, pointing to the bindings on her skis. "Was this another one of your planned 'accidents'?"

"Nope," Dave said, holding up his hands. He shook his head and leaned forward on his poles to look at the bindings. "I didn't have anything to do with that."

Nancy narrowed her eyes. "Were you anywhere near the skating pond last night?" she asked.

"Nope," Dave repeated. "Why?"

"Someone knocked me cold, and since you've admitted to the other accidents, I thought maybe you were responsible for that one, too," she said.

"I wasn't near the place." Dave actually smiled now. "Looks like I'm not the only one who wants to give you a hard time, eh?"

Nancy didn't think he was funny. She wasn't sure he was telling the truth. But if he was, there was still another criminal to catch. She kicked at the snow and thought out loud. "You wanted me to give Tall Pines a bad write-up. Why? Was your stealing the payroll cash part of your plan to cause trouble at Tall Pines, too?"

"I didn't have anything to do with the theft," Dave said, suddenly very serious again. "As far as I know, Rebecca Montgomery took the money."

"Rebecca denies it, and I believe her." Nancy told him that Rebecca was the reason she was at Tall Pines. "I honestly believe she's innocent. In fact, I still think Rob masterminded the theft and you were his accomplice."

"What?" Dave's face reflected his shock. "You've got to be kidding."

"No, I'm not. It's hardly a secret that Rob is making major improvements at his camp. How's he paying for them?" Nancy looked at Dave for a moment before she said, "I saw the file you have on Rob in your office, and I know how little money he makes. I think you and Rob decided that an extra fifty thousand dollars would help him nicely."

"Look, Nancy, I had nothing to do with that robbery, and neither did Rob." Dave's voice was low and insistent. "I admit I engineered those accidents, but I didn't steal anything."

"Where did Rob get the money for the construction?" Nancy asked.

"The same place most people do—the bank. He took out a huge construction loan. I thought he was crazy to start a big project, but sometimes you can't talk sense to Rob."

Nancy watched as a clump of snow slid down a pine bough and landed on the ground. "What's between you and Rob, anyway? When did you get to be such good friends? I doubt Karl Reismueller will be happy to hear about your friendship," she concluded.

Dave was hesitant but finally spoke up. "No, Karl wouldn't be too happy, especially if he found out I work for Rob Watson," he said.

"You work for Watson?" Nancy asked, stunned by the news.

"Yep." Dave pressed his lips together. "I know it sounds a little sleazy, and I guess it is. When Rob heard about Karl's plan to open Tall Pines, he asked me to get a job here and do what I could to sabotage the place. Then, when I told him a reporter was coming to review Tall Pines, he thought it was the perfect opportunity. He told me to make sure you gave Tall Pines a bad write-up. What better way than to make you miserable while you were here?"

Shaking her head in disgust, Nancy said, "That's pretty low."

"The resort business is competitive, but as in any other business, people don't always compete honestly," Dave said with a shrug. "But I didn't steal that money, and I don't know a thing about your bindings, or who knocked you out cold, or that missing file you keep talking about. That's the truth." He laughed a little. "I know you don't have any reason to believe me, but I am leveling with you."

With that Dave picked up Nancy's broken ski and studied the binding. "I think I can fix this good enough to get you down the trail," he said, pulling out a pocket knife. As Nancy watched, Dave moved another screw to the front of the binding.

"You'll have to go slowly," he told her, "but it will sure beat walking."

Nancy hooked her boots into the bindings and tried to glide. Though she felt a slight wobbling, the skis seemed reasonably secure.

"I think it'll be okay," she told Dave. "Thanks."

He stepped into his own bindings and slid his hands into the pole straps. "I'm not proud of my part in this," he said as he skied in the tracks next to Nancy. "When I get back I promise I'll tell Karl I quit. I hope you can keep it quiet about your 'accidents.' I really can assure you that I never meant to harm you."

"I'm glad to hear you say that," Nancy said. "Because if you weren't quitting, I would have to press charges against you. I'd suggest you clear out as soon as you can."

When they reached the bottom of the trail Nancy returned her skis to the shop, her mind fully occupied. The fact that Dave Kendall was only partially responsible for what had been happening at Tall Pines was frustrating news. It meant that Nancy still had to discover who had knocked her out, sabotaged her skis, and stolen the payroll money. It also failed to explain who Sheila's mystery man was or who had taken the missing bank file.

Nancy was about to find Jody Ashton's home address when her name was paged over the intercom. She picked up a house telephone on the ski school counter and told the operator she was ready for the call. In a second Chief McGinnis's voice came through.

"You were right, Nancy," the police chief told her. "One of those people does have a record. She was picked up for grand theft auto."

Theft. It was what Nancy had expected, the repetition of a crime pattern.

"Who was it?" she asked. "Sheila Reismueller?"

"No, Nancy. Sheila's clean. Your car thief is Jody Ashton."

Chapter

Fifteen

NANCY HUNG UP the phone, her mind whirling. Jody had left her the skis with the faulty bindings. Part of Jody's employment application was missing from the files—probably in order to hide her criminal past. Although she claimed to be saving for college, Jody had just bought a brand-new car.

"Nancy?" It was Dave Kendall. He had just come in and was standing next to her, a concerned expression on his face. "Is everything okay?"

After letting out a deep breath, Nancy nodded and took out her notebook from her belt pack. "I'm fine. Look—I need a favor."

"Anything. I owe you at least one." He leaned toward Nancy and whispered, "Thanks for being so understanding about what I did," he said.

"It's between you and Karl when you leave," Nancy said. She grabbed a pencil from her belt pack and said, "I need to know Jody Ashton's address."

Dave picked up the house phone and waited for the operator to answer. Within a few minutes he'd gotten Jody's address and phone number for Nancy.

Nancy thanked him and headed out of the ski shop and toward her condo. Once she got there she tried calling Jody's house, but there was no answer. She also called the Marvins' again, but no one was home there, either. Sighing, Nancy picked up the flashlight and stashed it in her purse. The flashlight might prove useful if she needed to get a confession out of Jody. Nancy was sure she'd smelled Sheila's perfume in the building, but there was a chance—however slim —that Jody had been the one to knock her out.

When Nancy reached Monroe ten minutes later it was just noon. She drove through the main shopping area and stopped at a gas station to ask for directions to Jody's street. The brand-new green sports car was parked in front of the building, so Nancy knew that the girl was home.

Nancy parked her Mustang and found Jody's apartment listed on the directory.

"Hi, Nancy." Jody gave her a friendly if confused smile. "What brings you here?"

"Can I come in?" Nancy asked. As she stepped inside Nancy found herself surprised by Jody's reaction. If Jody had loosened the ski bindings, she should have been startled—even shocked— to see her.

"Those were some skis you left me," Nancy said casually, her hands in her jacket pockets.

"What skis?" Jody seemed to be puzzled.

"The ones with the new bindings."

Jody frowned. "I know I promised you new skis, but the shipment didn't come in before I left yesterday. I'm hoping it'll be there when I go back tomorrow."

Nancy wondered if Jody could be as innocent as she was acting. If she was, Nancy was obviously on the wrong track. "Jody, Ben gave me new skis with a note from you," she said.

This time Jody made no attempt to hide her confusion. "But I didn't write any note—I don't know what you're talking about."

Nancy felt for the note in her jacket pocket, took it out, and handed it to Jody. "That's not your signature?" she asked.

"No," Jody said, slowly reading over the note. She grabbed her purse from the coffee table, pulled out a pen, and scrawled her name on the note. Sure enough, the looping script was not at all similar to the angular signature on the typed note.

"I wasn't even at Tall Pines today," Jody went on. "How could I have left you those skis? Why are you asking all these questions anyway?"

Nancy took the note back from Jody and went to sit on a cream love seat in the middle of the living room.

"Someone loosened the bindings on one of the

skis I thought you'd left me," Nancy told her. "I was out on the trails and nearly had a very serious accident."

Jody blanched. "You think *I* did it?" There was a note of outrage in her voice.

"I think you could have," Nancy answered.

"But why would I?"

Nancy decided to make her answer completely straightforward. "To keep me from finding out that you stole the payroll money."

"What?" Jody began to pace her living room, her green eyes alive with anger. "I didn't steal any money! Rebecca did that."

"Rebecca was framed," Nancy said evenly. "You're my number-one suspect."

Jody stopped pacing and was silent for a long minute. When she spoke her face was pale. "What makes you say that?" she asked in a low voice that had a slight quaver.

"First of all, there's the unexplained money," Nancy said. She leaned forward on the couch, resting her forearms on her knees. "You told me how much you needed money for college, then you showed up in a new sports car. One explanation is that you used money you stole from Tall Pines for your car."

Two red spots appeared on Jody's cheeks. "I didn't take the money," she declared.

"Jody," Nancy said slowly, "I know about your car theft conviction."

When Jody spoke her voice was seething with anger. "That's over!" she cried. "I paid for that, and believe me I learned my lesson."

"What happened exactly?" Nancy asked.

Jody sat down in an armchair across from Nancy. When she spoke it was so quietly that Nancy had to strain to hear her words. "A friend and I took her father's car for a joyride one night. We got into an accident and did some damage to the car. I don't know why, but he pressed criminal charges against me. It was booked as grand theft auto, and since I was driving when we got caught, I took the whole rap." Jody shuddered as she recounted her experience. "I got a light sentence, but even so, it was not pleasant. I'll *never* steal again."

There was no doubting Jody's sincerity. Nancy remembered how violently Jody had reacted when she'd first mentioned the theft, and how Jody had declared that Rebecca deserved what she'd gotten. Now that Nancy knew Jody's background she could understand the outburst. She'd paid for her crime. If Rebecca was the thief, Jody felt that she should do the same.

"What about the Corvette?" Nancy asked. "Where'd you get the money for that?"

"The car was a mistake," Jody admitted, grimacing. "I thought I wanted it more than anything else, so I decided to use my college money for the down payment. Now that I've got it, I've realized that college is more important than any car. Luckily the dealer gave it to me on a two-day trial. I'm taking it back this afternoon."

Nancy flashed Jody a reassuring smile. "I think that's a good decision." She paused. There was just one more thing Nancy had to be sure of before she completely ruled Jody out as a suspect. She pulled the flashlight from her purse. "Ever see this before?" she asked.

"Looks like an ordinary flashlight to me," Jody said with a shrug. Then she leaned closer to get a better look. "Wait a minute." Taking the flashlight from Nancy, Jody touched the cracked lens. "This is Karl's," she said. "How did you get it?"

"Karl's!" Nancy exclaimed. "Karl Reismueller's? Are you sure?"

"Of course I'm sure." Jody leaned back in the chair, a smile on her lips. "I've seen him use it. I even kidded him about it once. He said he was too busy to get it fixed." She made a wry smile. "If I had as much money as Karl does, I think I'd just throw it away and get a new one."

So it was Karl Reismueller who'd knocked her out—or someone using Karl's flashlight. All Nancy's reasons to suspect Jody were now gone. All, that is, except for the missing bank file.

"Jody, I have just one more question," Nancy said.

"Shoot," said Jody.

"Did you have any reason to take a file of bank records from Dave Kendall's office?" she asked.

Jody squinted, obviously thinking about Nancy's question. "No." She shrugged. "But if there's something you need to know, I'm good friends with Alyssa Shelly, one of the managers at Monroe Savings and Loan."

Nancy practically hugged the girl. "Perfect. Do me a favor and tell her I'm coming down to ask her a few questions." Nancy waited while Jody made the call. When the girl finished, Nancy said, "I'm sorry I had to ask you so many embarrassing questions. I hope you understand why I thought what I did."

"Don't worry," Jody said. She tossed her auburn curls and smiled. "It's not the first time that stupid mistake has haunted me."

Jody walked outside with Nancy. "I want to return this car before anything happens to it," she said, sighing as they came up to it. "It's beautiful, but to tell you the truth, driving such an expensive car makes me nervous."

Nancy waved goodbye and drove off in the direction of the bank. Along the way she spotted a public phone and decided to try calling the Marvins' one more time.

"I don't understand this whole thing," Bess's mother said when she answered the phone. "Mr. Marvin and I got a phone call this morning telling us to go to the hospital. We hurried over there to find Bess. At the same time Bess was here looking for us."

Nancy frowned.

"Are George and Bess there now?" she asked.

"No," Mrs. Marvin answered. "They drove back up to Tall Pines. Bess said they wanted to help you with your investigation."

As she got back into the Mustang Nancy was relieved that everything was okay, but also worried. The same person had obviously called both Bess and her parents and given them conflicting messages. Was that person Sheila Reismueller? If so, why had she wanted Bess and George out of the way?

The traffic light was red. While she waited for it to turn green Nancy glanced at the stores around her. A short man in a black and white houndstooth suit and a black fedora stopped in front of one of the stores. Reaching into his pocket, he drew out a key and unlocked the door. Nancy stared at him and knew there was no doubt. He was the same man she'd seen with Sheila!

When the light turned green Nancy found a parking spot, got out of her car, and hurried over to the shop. Sam's Pawnshop, the sign said.

The thought of the Reismuellers' financial problems stuck in Nancy's mind as she went in and scanned the shop. Every imaginable item from household appliances to ice skates was arranged on shelves that stretched from floor to ceiling. Were the Reismuellers' problems so bad that Sheila had to pawn something of hers— something valuable?

"Can I help you, miss?" the man in the houndstooth suit asked. Without his fedora he didn't look half so distinguished. His hair was greased back, his eyes were bloodshot, and his hands were long, thin, and bony. "What are you looking for?"

"Do you have any diamond pins?" she asked, knowing it was a shot in the dark.

The man unlocked a drawer behind the counter and pulled out two pins on a velvet-covered tray. "The starburst is nice," he said, "but this other one is one of a kind."

Nancy drew in a deep breath as the man handed her the very same diamond horseshoe pin that had once been Sheila Reismueller's favorite.

"This is beautiful," she said as she held the horseshoe, "but I think you must be mistaken. I'm sure I've seen another one like it."

"No, miss," the man said quickly. "The owner had it made specially for her. I know. I bought it from her myself."

"And how long ago was that?" Nancy asked, turning the pin over in her hands. On the back the initials *SR* were engraved. It had to be Sheila's!

"Just a couple of days ago. I have some more jewelry from the same woman—if you'd care to see it." Nancy shook her head as the man took the pin from her. "Will you be wanting to buy this, then?"

Nancy tried to hide her smile of satisfaction. The pawnbroker had just confirmed her suspicions. "I'll think about it," she said.

The man nodded, putting the pin back on its velvet tray. "Come back and see me when you've made up your mind."

Nancy thanked him and left. As she closed the pawnshop door behind her she felt her excitement building. Sheila had obviously met the man at least twice. Now the question was, did Sheila steal the payroll to help Karl, or was that all Karl's doing?

Two blocks later Nancy pulled her car up in front of the Monroe Savings and Loan. After a few minutes she was sitting at Alyssa Shelly's desk and explaining to the manager who she was.

"I realize this may be confidential information," Nancy said, meeting the woman's soft brown eyes. "But there are a few things I need to know about the resort's finances."

Alyssa Shelly clasped her hands on her desk. "What kind of information?"

"Is Tall Pines sound financially?" Nancy asked. "I mean, would an investor, say, have any reason to doubt she'd put her money in a solid venture?"

Alyssa gave Nancy an apologetic smile. "I'm sorry, but I really can't give out that kind of information."

Nancy thought for a moment. "Can you at least tell me whether Karl Reismueller has any outstanding loans with your bank?"

After a moment Alyssa nodded. "Yes, he does."

Leaning forward in her chair, Nancy said, "Just tell me if I'm right about something. I have a feeling Karl has been late with his payments lately, but that suddenly—say, just about three and a half weeks ago—he made a payment of forty-eight thousand dollars." Studying Alyssa closely, she asked, "Do your records back that up?"

Alyssa glanced through the papers in the file on

her desk. "I'd say those are pretty good guesses," she said with a smile. She hastened to add, "I can't confirm that officially, though."

Grinning, Nancy thanked Alyssa for her help. That was all the proof she needed. Karl Reismueller was definitely her man.

Chapter

Sixteen

KARL DID IT, Nancy thought as she drove back to Tall Pines. As strange as it seemed, he had stolen money from his own company to make the loan payments. From the files she'd seen on the computer, Nancy knew that the expense of opening Tall Pines had drained him of cash. Now she knew he'd been in danger of losing the resort. Karl was obviously willing to do anything to keep the resort running.

Nancy parked her car next to her condo and raced inside. She wanted to call Bess and George to tell them what she knew. When she placed the call she found out the cousins weren't back yet. As soon as she hung up the phone, it rang. The operator came on the line and told her Karl had left a message asking her to find him on the Cascades trail. Nancy thanked her and hung up.

Great, Nancy thought. That saved her the trouble of looking for him. Before leaving to meet Karl Nancy called and left a message for Bess and George telling them where she'd be.

With that Nancy picked up her old skis and headed to the trail head. Karl hadn't said where on the trail he would meet her, but she ran into Ben as he was coming out of the ski shop.

"Karl told me to meet him on the Cascades trail," she told him. "Do you have any idea where on the trail I should try?"

Ben shrugged. "That's odd. I know he does like the view near the hut where Cascades and Aerie meet. He might have gone there."

"Thanks." Nancy flashed Ben a quick smile, put on her bindings, and headed up Aerie, which she knew would be the fastest way to get to the small hut. As she skied she felt a chill and wondered why she was going off alone to meet Karl. It seemed strange that he wanted her to find him on the trail. Given what she knew about Karl and his deceptions, she knew she shouldn't trust the man. Still, she wanted to confront him with what she knew, and the sooner she did that, the better.

The sun was beginning to set. If Nancy hadn't been so worried about finding Karl, she would have enjoyed the view. The fiery red ball of a sun appeared to be suspended among the pines, and the growing darkness cast a mysterious pink glow over the trail.

Nancy had no time to admire it, though. Her

arms and legs were moving in a smooth and steady rhythm as she forced each stride to take her farther and faster.

When she first saw Karl he was only a speck in the distance. For a few minutes she wasn't even sure it was him. Then he turned slightly, and she recognized his profile. The man was definitely Karl Reismueller.

He was skiing more slowly than Nancy. As she drew closer Karl stopped. It took only a few more glides for Nancy to reach the man's side.

"We've got to talk." Her words came out in short bursts as she tried to catch her breath.

In a movement so swift she had no way of anticipating it, Karl grabbed Nancy's arm.

"I don't think there's anything to talk about," he snarled. "You've meddled once too often. This time you're not going to get away with it."

Nancy jerked her arm, trying to break loose from Karl, but she had no success.

"You're going to have an unfortunate accident." Karl laughed, and the sound sent shivers up Nancy's spine. There was no mirth in his laughter, only evil pleasure.

Suddenly he released her arm. "Stay next to me," he ordered. "Don't even think about getting away."

Nancy took a deep breath, trying to quell her fear. She leaned forward on her poles and pushed off. In that split second she had the advantage of surprise. When Karl had grabbed her arm he had dropped his poles, leaving them hanging by the straps around his wrists. It took him a few precious seconds to grip the poles and begin to ski. Those seconds were all Nancy needed.

She skied off the trail and into the forest. On the Aerie trail, with its double set of tracks, she'd have no chance of escaping Karl. Here she'd have the protection of the trees. Their trunks were so close together that only one skier could move comfortably between them. It would be more difficult for Karl to catch her.

Nancy kept her poles close to her side, bending over slightly to gain more power. Her arms and legs moved rhythmically, and her skis glided smoothly over the packed snow.

"You can't escape!" Karl's voice came from a distance.

Nancy refused to turn around. It would break her stride, costing her valuable seconds. She forced her arms to stretch even farther, propelling her skis forward.

"Give up, Nancy! You can't win." This time Karl's voice sounded closer.

Nancy shifted her weight to her right ski, turning sharply around a large pine tree. She needed a plan of escape. Her eyes moved quickly across the horizon. The forest thinned, and she could see a clearing. Was that dark spot a building?

"You'll never outski me," Karl taunted. There was no doubt that he was gaining on her. This time his voice sounded as though he was only a few yards behind her.

Nancy strained as she tried to identify the dark spot. It *was* a building! She recognized the small hut where the trails divided. The building could be a safe haven. She had to reach it before Karl.

"Give up, Nancy! You have no chance."

The hut was in sight. Though every muscle in her arms and legs burned from exertion, Nancy forced them to move even more quickly. She was almost there.

"You fool!" Nancy could hear the swish of Karl's skis. He was close now, dangerously close.

She turned for the first time. He was only ten feet behind her, grinning as though he had no doubt he'd win.

Now! It had to be now!

Nancy gripped both poles. With a quick twist of her wrists she planted the poles on her binding release buttons. Then, before Karl realized what was happening, she stepped out of her skis.

"Stop!" he yelled.

He was too late. Nancy ran into the hut and slammed the door behind her.

She reached to slide the bolt shut, but her hand hit the flat wooden surface of the door. There was no bolt! With a cry of frustration Nancy realized she was trapped. With no way to lock the door, it would be only seconds before Karl broke in.

"That was very stupid, Nancy Drew." Karl shoved the door open and stood in the doorway. He reached into his pocket and drew out a gun.

Nancy stared at the gun and felt cold fear in the pit of her stomach. "You won't get away with it," she said, trying to keep her voice low and steady.

Karl took another step into the room and slammed the door behind him. "Who's going to stop me once you're gone?" he asked. The light of the fading sun streamed through the one window, and Nancy could see Karl's grin. "It's a shame your little accident this morning didn't finish you off."

She had to keep him talking. That would give her time to think of a plan. "So you were the one who fixed my bindings," Nancy said. "That was clever. If I had been hurt or killed, it would have looked like an accident."

Karl shrugged and trained the gun on her. "If it didn't, Jody would have taken the blame." He gave Nancy a long, appraising look. "I kept another copy of the note I wrote, just in case you threw the first one away. I had the story all planned. It's even better than the one you were supposed to be writing for *Tracks*. Want to hear my story?" Karl asked. "Jody found out you were a detective. She didn't want anyone to know about her stealing the money, so she arranged a little skiing accident."

Unfortunately, Nancy knew Karl had a story someone—even the police—might believe.

"Very nice," Nancy said. "I still don't know how you found out I was a detective."

"You're not the only one who knows how to investigate," Karl told her. "Your name sounded familiar, so I did some checking with people I knew in River Heights. They told me who you were. A quick call to *Tracks* confirmed it all. That's when I put two and two together about you and your friends. You were quite a trio. Isn't it a shame you won't see them again?"

For the first time Nancy felt real fear. "What did you do to George and Bess?" she demanded.

Karl laughed. "Don't worry. It was nothing permanent. Without you, they're no threat. I just got them out of the way today." He paused, cocked his eyebrow at her, and glanced at the gun he was holding. "I told you I planned everything. The only thing I didn't plan was that you'd walk away from your little skiing accident this morning."

Karl took another step toward Nancy. "When Sheila told me you were asking a lot of questions I started worrying. Then I happened to be passing by the administration building last night and saw you and your friend come out. That was when I knew I had to get rid of you."

"That wasn't very smart, leaving your flashlight in the snack bar," Nancy told him.

Karl made no attempt to deny Nancy's accusation. "I didn't plan to leave it," he said, "but I heard Sheila coming, and I didn't want her to know I was there. I slipped out before she saw me."

Nancy had to keep him talking while her mind raced for a plan. The door behind Karl was swinging in the wind. If she could just get past him, she might be able to escape.

"And you're willing to risk a murder rap just to cover up a theft?" Nancy asked, pointing at the gun in Karl's hand.

"You don't understand, do you, Nancy Drew?" Karl's voice was low and angry. "I was the man with the Midas touch. Everyone considered me a genius. People were always calling and asking for my opinion. Then things started to fall apart. Tall Pines cost a lot more than I'd planned, and we had a bad season at the toy stores. Suddenly the famous Karl Reismueller money machine wasn't making money anymore."

Karl's voice grew harsh. "I couldn't let anyone know. It would destroy my reputation."

"So you stole money from your own company."

Karl laughed. "I told you I was brilliant, didn't I? It was easy. The insurance company covered most of the loss, so I walked away with almost fifty thousand dollars."

Karl glanced at his watch. "We've wasted too much time," he said matter-of-factly.

With that, Karl cocked the gun.

"Nancy Drew, you've got to die."

Chapter
Seventeen

NANCY DREW IN a sharp breath. The sound of the gun's cocking echoed in her ears. Karl was truly serious. He *was* going to kill her!

"How will you explain a gunshot wound?" she asked, swallowing hard and trying to hide her fear. "No one will believe it was an accident."

Karl laughed. "Of course they won't! I'm smarter than that. The gun's only to make sure you ski over the cliff." He shook his head sadly. "It will be such an unfortunate accident. I may even close the trail for the rest of the season so that none of the other guests will be in danger." Karl's low chuckle made Nancy's skin crawl.

"People know I'm a good skier," Nancy said. To her own ears her voice sounded quite desperate. She hoped Karl couldn't tell. "No one will believe I skied off a cliff."

Karl wasn't interested in conversation. "Stop

stalling," he ordered. His empty hand pointed toward the door. "Out! It's time for you to take a little fall."

Nancy stepped toward the door. Karl was waiting for her to go out ahead of him. Just as she was passing him Nancy seized her only opportunity. She shot her leg out in the quick reflexive kick she'd been taught in her martial arts classes.

It worked! The gun went spinning out of Karl's hand and landed on the floor. Nancy lunged, tackling Karl with all her might. Though he was a big man, he wasn't prepared for the sudden attack. Surprise and skill were on Nancy's side, and he fell easily to the ground.

The gun lay on the floor two feet from Karl's outstretched hand. Nancy moved quickly, reaching for it. But her luck ran out. The older man was too swift. He grabbed Nancy's ankle and yanked her off balance.

"I'm going to kill you!" he cried as he wrestled with Nancy, trying to pin her to the floor. Although Karl far outweighed Nancy, she had the advantage of agility and cunning. She struggled against him, trying to keep him away from the gun. She twisted—hard—out of his grasp and rolled away from him. At that very moment the door swung open, and George and Ben burst into the room.

"Need a little help?" Ben asked.

For an instant Karl was so surprised that he didn't move. It was the break Nancy needed. She launched herself at Karl, forcing him back down on the floor.

George moved quickly to the side of the room. "I've got the gun," she announced, and she pointed it at Karl.

"Thanks, guys," Nancy said as she jumped to her feet. "Your timing was perfect."

"Are you sure they're all coming?" Sheila's voice quavered with emotion, and she drummed her fingers on the arm of the wingback chair. Though she was once again at home in her condo, it was obvious that she was still reliving the events of the previous evening.

"They'll be here," Nancy assured her.

Nancy had driven Sheila to the police station the night before and stayed with her while Karl was booked on charges of defrauding the insurance company, theft, and attempted murder.

"I still can't believe Karl did all that," Sheila said. "Of course, he never really confided in me about his business. Whenever I asked he told me it was complicated, and I wouldn't understand."

"But you did pawn your diamonds, Sheila. You must have known Tall Pines needed money."

"Karl told me we had minor cash-flow problems," Sheila explained. "I thought the quick money I'd get from selling my jewelry would help. But I had no idea he was in so deep or that he'd consider stealing." She hid her face in her hands. "Oh, Karl," Sheila said. When she looked up at Nancy there were tears in her crystal blue eyes. "It's a terrible thing when your husband's ambition turns him into a criminal."

Nancy felt bad for the woman. She obviously

had no idea of the awful things Karl was capable of. "I'm just glad George and Bess got back in time to save me," she said.

"You were very lucky," Sheila agreed. "How can I ever apologize to you for what has happened here?"

A brisk knock on the door prevented Nancy from answering. Sheila hesitated, then rose to her feet and opened it. "Come in," she said.

George and Bess were followed by Rebecca, Ben, and Jody. When everyone was seated Sheila leaned forward in her chair. Her blue eyes were serious, and her lips trembled as she began to speak.

"I asked you all to come here," she said, "because I wanted to apologize for everything that's happened. Even though I didn't take part in the things that Karl did, I do feel responsible. You see, Tall Pines was my dream. If it hadn't been for me, Karl would never have built the resort."

"It was a wonderful dream," Bess said. "This is the best resort I've ever seen."

Sheila managed a small smile. Then she turned to Rebecca. "I'm so sorry for what we put you through. I hope you'll take your job back."

Rebecca's grin was the only answer anyone needed. "I'll be back at work first thing tomorrow," she announced.

George shot Rebecca a conspiratorial look. "See," she said. "I told you Nancy would help."

There was one more question Nancy wanted answered. "Were you by any chance responsible for a page being missing from Jody's personnel file?" she asked Ben.

He flushed. "I was afraid you'd find out about Jody's conviction and put it in your article, so I destroyed that page."

The last pieces fit into the puzzle.

"You've been a great manager," Sheila told Jody. "The gift shop is booming, and so is the ski shop. I think you have the qualities I need in a general manager. Do you think you could handle the job?"

"You bet I could!" Jody exclaimed, her eyes widening.

"Then it's settled." Looking at Ben, Sheila added, "I'm going to hire a painter."

"A painter? Why do you need a painter?" he asked.

This time Sheila chuckled. "To letter the new sign. You know, the one that will say the Ben Wrobley Ski School."

Before Ben could react George cried, "That's great! It sounds so much better than the Inge Gustafson School."

"I'm glad you said that," Ben said with a laugh. "It would sound conceited coming from me."

"Of course, there's a pay raise that goes along with the new sign," Sheila pointed out. "You may have to wait a bit until I sell all our other assets, but even with the expense of Karl's defense I think I'll be able to manage raises."

A broad grin creased Ben's face. "That sounds even better than the sign." He leaned forward and smiled at Nancy. "And to make up for what you've been through, Nancy, I'll be glad to give you a season's free skiing lessons."

Nancy glanced at Sheila, Rebecca, George, and Bess before she answered Ben. "No, thanks," she said with a grin. "I think I'll try a less dangerous sport—something like hang gliding."

Nancy's next case:

Five years have passed since the tragic car crash that took the life of country-western great Curtis Taylor. Nancy visits his hometown—site of a concert in his honor—to investigate a report that Taylor has been seen alive. But she determines not only that he's dead, but that he may have been murdered!

The concert is a tabloid newspaper's dream: Greed, jealousy, and backstabbing have stolen the show. Taylor's widow, his nephew, his former manager . . . everyone involved has a tale to tell. But Nancy's after the one person hiding in the wings—an elusive murderer still at large . . . in *FINAL NOTES*, Case #65 in The Nancy Drew Files℠.

THE HARDY BOYS® CASE FILES